The
Haunting
Of
Owl Creek

Chapter 1

Ellen had always dreamed of adventure, of travelling to exotic places and meeting exciting people. She had struggled through high school with a promise to herself that, after graduation, she would leave her hometown of Wood Hollow, Ohio and find happiness in another place far, far away.

Her wanderlust, however, was cured by a healthy dose of reality in the form of a baby girl. She had become pregnant after a heated summer affair with Joey Jacobs, a boy born to trouble that ended up in prison for armed robbery when she was just three months pregnant. Thus, her unborn child was, for the most part, fatherless, and she was forced to grow up fast and without any guidance.

Her mother had passed away three years before from breast cancer and her father, a long-time drunk, had left town when she was only seven years old. Her father's sister had cared for her out of obligation until she was eighteen, but then she was on her own.

So, at the ripe age of eighteen, on the brink of womanhood, when she found herself in the family way, she quickly located a job at a small law firm, answering phones and filing documents. The pay was lousy, but it was enough for her to afford a run-down apartment on the West Side of town in the low-rent district. The apartment, located on Summit Avenue, was small, the heat was closely monitored and kept just above freezing, and the parking was minimal, but it provided her shelter from the frigid winters and a place to call home.

The neighborhood consisted mainly of unsavory characters with criminal backgrounds and unemployed individuals with gambling and drug habits, but there were a few decent, hard-working people, as well.

As luck would have it, one such decent person lived just two doors down from her in 3b. Kathryn Callahan was a retired secretary whose husband had died unexpectedly at the age of forty-five. He had not felt a life insurance policy was a wise investment, so, upon his untimely death, Kathryn had been left with an endless pile of unpaid hospital bills and was forced to sell their house and move to Summit Avenue.

When Ellen's baby was born, Kathryn, who never had any children of her own due to a medical condition, offered to care for the child for a small, weekly stipend. Naturally, Ellen was delighted to have such a lovely, responsible woman to care for her child.

Ellen named the baby Natalie, after her mother. When Natalie was just a few months old Ellen decided to go to college, as her job at the law firm didn't offer much room for advancement without a degree. Her boss, Andrew Simpson, had offered to pay for her tuition if she agreed to stay with the firm for two years after graduation. She agreed to the arrangement and began attending Mt. Vernon Technical College. It was a two-year college and she elected to take evening courses in hopes of becoming a paralegal.

Fortunately, the college offered a childcare program for working adults, so Ellen had someone to care for Natalie both during the day while she was working and at night, while she was in class. This arrangement worked well, but left Ellen both physically and mentally exhausted. Between her job and the endless supply of essays and term papers, she had little time for a social life.

Every once in a while, she would meet her one and only friend, Marcie, for lunch or dinner. On one such occasion, she had agreed to meet Marcie at Zarraco's, a small, quaint restaurant that served anything from Double Decker's to filet mignon. Marcie, a flight attendant, was seldom in town and claimed to have some exciting information to share, so Ellen made the necessary childcare arrangements and rushed to Zarraco's after work.

Upon entering the restaurant, Ellen spotted her friend sitting in a corner booth. Although she loved Marcie dearly, she couldn't help but feel a twinge of jealousy at the sight of her friend. Tall and slender, with big blue eyes, stylish, long, blonde hair, and perfectly applied make-up, Marcie was nothing short of gorgeous. Not to mention, she had a glamorous life, flying all over the world and meeting new and exciting people all the time.

Approaching the table, Ellen smiled brightly at her friend, "Hey, Marcie! It's so good to see you!"

Marcie jumped up and flung her arms around her friend. "Oh, my God! Ellen, you look great! Did you do something different with your hair? It's darker, right?"

Ellen smiled again. Marcie was always full of compliments and praise. Though she had curled her hair and applied make-up, Ellen hardly thought she looked great. Still, the compliment from her friend lifted her spirits.

After placing their orders, Ellen asked Marcie what her exciting news was about. Marcie, always prone to dramatics, made a great show of a sparkling diamond engagement ring adorning her left ring finger. Ellen, who's most exciting news lately was the "A" she had managed to get in her Business Ethics class and the fact that Natalie would finally eat carrots, was happy for her friend.

Marcie shared with Ellen that the man who gave her the ring was a pilot, and they were going to be wed in the spring. Although neither of them knew it at the time, the pilot in question was actually already married with three kids and had no plans of leaving his wife, but for the moment the two women talked of wedding plans over hamburgers and beer and laughed like schoolgirls. Ellen hadn't had so much fun in what seemed like an eternity.

On her way home, on a whim, she stopped at a local coffeehouse. She planned to surprise Kathryn, who was watching Natalie that evening, with lattes and fresh baked cookies. Despite the seemingly late hour (it was after 9:00pm), the coffeehouse was in full swing, and Ellen was forced to wait in, what appeared from her vantage point, to be an endless line of customers, eager to get their late-night caffeine fix.

Before long, the man in front of her, a tall, slender fellow dressed in a dark sweater and khakis, turned to ask her the time. She glanced at her watch and turned her gaze upwards to inform the man that it was ten after nine. Ellen was taken aback by the intense blue abyss that were his eyes. She stood there, staring at him, unable to move or speak, lost in his hypnotic gaze. After a while, the man, whom by this time Ellen had noticed was painfully handsome, politely asked again for the time.

Ellen, realizing that she appeared rude, quickly, in a somewhat shaky voice, reported the time, "Um, it's eleven after nine."

He smiled, thanked her, and turned back around to continue to wait for his chance to place an order at the ever-distant counter.

As Ellen continued to stand there, criticizing herself for acting such a fool when confronted by an attractive man, one of the two teenage boys behind her took that precise moment to push his friend, rather roughly, right into the back of Ellen. Caught off guard, she stumbled forward, smack dab into Mr. Blue Eyes. He, in turn, pitched forward, as well. Fortunately, neither of them actually hit the floor, as there was a small, Formica table that broke their fall. Ellen's purse, however, was less fortunate, and its contents spilled all over the black and white linoleum floor, littering the tiles with lipsticks, mascara, checkbook and God forbid, tampons.

As Ellen frantically attempted to collect the discarded items of her purse, Mr. Blue Eyes regained his composure and offered to assist her. Ellen was mortified when he bent down to pick up a stray tampon that had landed by his left loafer. Barely concealing a smile, he handed it to her. She snatched the offending tampon from his grasp and stuffed it into the deep recesses of her purse, certain, that at any moment, she would be the first person in recorded history, to die of embarrassment.

Attempting to pretend as though nothing had happened that could be construed, in the least way, as utterly humiliating, Ellen casually stepped back into line, but not before shooting a rather nasty glance at the teenage boys behind her. Sullenly, they dropped their heads and stared at the floor. She was satisfied that they felt guilty and accepted their averted gazes as an apology for their juvenile actions.

By this time, the line had moved surprisingly forward, and Ellen noticed that Mr. Blue Eyes was placing his order in front of her. Graciously, he turned to her and asked if he could buy her a coffee or cappuccino. Hesitantly, she explained that she was actually purchasing lattes for herself and a friend and didn't expect him to pay for them. He said he didn't mind and placed the order.

While they waited, he asked her name, which she obligingly told him. He commented that her name was pretty, but she was certain he was just being polite. Then, she remembered her manners and asked his name. He told her it was Scott Christianson. He explained that he worked in insurance sales and then, unexpectedly, he asked if she would like to go to dinner sometime. She was completely taken aback by his proposal and didn't immediately answer. After careful consideration, she agreed and gave him her phone number, which he jotted down on a napkin. They parted ways then, and he promised to call her soon.

As she walked home, she couldn't help feeling elated. Despite all the setbacks in her life, she was hopeful that she could start afresh. After all, she would finish school soon, perhaps receive a promotion at work, move away from Summit Avenue, and maybe, just maybe, start a relationship with, quite possibly, the most handsome man she had ever met.

Chapter 2

"Whatcha doing?" Scott asked his wife. He had just come home from a grueling day at the office. He stood in the doorway of their bedroom, staring at Ellen who was sprawled on the bed, their wedding album open in front of her.

Rolling onto her back, she lazily stretched her body, which had become cramped from being in the same position for too long. She hadn't realized how long she had been reminiscing about the past and counting her blessings about the present.

Reaching her arms towards her husband, she indicated in that special way of hers that she wanted him to join her on the bed. He removed his shoes and dropped down beside her, placing one arm behind his head and the other around his wife's shoulders.

"I was just thinking of you, how we met." Ellen answered.

Scott chuckled, recalling their chance encounter in a small coffeehouse, since closed down, the owners forced to relocate to a better neighborhood due to the rising crime.

"Why did you ask me out?" Ellen wanted to know. She often asked this question, but no matter how many times he told her, she liked to hear his explanation time and time again.

"Because you were so cute and you seemed so lost, like a little puppy that's wandered too far from home. I wanted to take you home and tend to your every need." He told her.

She smiled at him, her brown eyes warming into molten chocolate. He turned so that he could kiss her, which he never grew tired of, each time seeming like the first time their lips met.

They had been married for a little over a year, having celebrated their one-year anniversary just two months before. It had been a delightful evening, one filled with champagne and celebration with friends and family. Ellen couldn't believe that she was this man's wife. Life couldn't get any better.

"I was thinking," Scott began. "Maybe it's time we found a house. You know, a place with a yard for Natalie to play in. She's getting older and we're outgrowing this apartment, don't you think?"

Ellen thought about this for a moment. Sure, the apartment was small, but it was their first place together. She wasn't so sure she was ready to leave just yet.

"I don't know, Scott. I mean, how will we afford a house? We just barely make enough money to cover the rent here. A house means a big mortgage, utility bills that we're not used to paying. There are all kinds of expenses in owning a house. Maybe we should wait until one of us gets a better job." She said.

"Well, I was hoping to take you out to dinner to tell you this, but now is as good a time as any, I suppose. You know that promotion I put in for at the office?" He waited, letting the excitement build.

"You got it!" Ellen exclaimed. She rolled over and straddled him, looking down at him expectantly, waiting for his reply.

"Yeah. John just told me today. I'm going to be making at least ten grand more a year. The extra money could help us get a house." Scott told her.

"Oh, Scott! I'm so happy for you. You really deserve this!" Ellen said, as she kissed him.

Just then, Natalie's voice interrupted the moment. "Mommy, I'm hungry. When's dinner ready?"

Scott gently pushed his wife aside and walked over to Natalie, picking her up and swinging her in the air the way she liked.

"Guess what, kiddo? We're going out for dinner tonight. You pick the place." He told her.

"Peppy's Pizza! I want to go to Peppy's for dinner!" she squealed.

"Well, then, Peppy's it is." Scott said.

Chapter 3

Two months later, Ellen was looking through the real estate section of the newspaper. Already, she had circled three houses that were within their budget, although none of them were in a very good school district. Natalie was four years old and would be starting kindergarten next year. The last thing Ellen wanted was for her only daughter to end up in a school full of delinquent children with miscreants for parents.

Just as she was about to give up her search, she spotted a picture of a house that had all the makings of a real home. Though the picture wasn't of the best quality, the image slightly blurred and in black and white, she could tell that the house had real character. She certainly was no expert on architecture, but she had picked up a thing or two since her house hunting began, and she felt this particular house was a Tudor.

From the picture, the house looked like it was old, maybe from the 1920's or older. She scanned the text below the picture, which, indeed, stated the house was built in 1911. The ad also said that the house had four bedrooms, two full baths, a basement, wood-burning fireplace, and was located on over two acres of wooded land.

The address was 621 Owl Creek Drive, which, Ellen knew, was located on the Upper East Side of Crescentville in Braxton County. This particular area of town was very nice, and the school district was a good one. Ellen continued to scan the ad until she came to the price. The ad said the house was listed for $120,000. Doubt began to creep over her. There was no possible way a house like the one described could ever be that cheap. She decided that it must be a misprint and tossed the newspaper aside, feeling dejected and hopeless.

Just then, she heard the familiar jingle of keys in the door. Scott must be home. It was Saturday morning and Scott had gone out to get groceries, which he always did on Saturday morning.

Ellen jumped up to help him with the packages, as he fumbled his way through the door, his arms loaded down with bags of bread, milk, and other household necessities. As they unpacked the groceries, Scott asked her if she had had any luck locating a house.

"Not really." Ellen answered, placing cans of alphabet soup, Natalie's favorite, in the cabinet above the sink. "There just isn't anything in our price range *and* in a good school district. I don't think we're ever going to find the right house."

"Don't be so pessimistic. Of course, we're going to find a house. It just takes time and we've only been looking for a couple of months. Are you sure there wasn't anything in the paper?" he asked.

"No. Well, there was this one house, but I think the price was printed wrong. It was in Crescentville, and you know those houses cost a fortune." Ellen answered.

"Well, how much did it say?" Scott wanted to know.

Rather than explain the whole thing, Ellen grabbed the paper from the kitchen table and handed it to him.

"It's at the bottom." She told him and continued to put away the groceries, certain her husband would agree that the price was a misprint. He just had to see it for himself.

Scott took the paper and leaned against the counter, mulling over the ad. After a moment, he said, "I think we should make an appointment to go see it."

"What? Are you insane? You know that house is out of our range. There's no way it's as cheap as the ad says." Ellen said, a little taken aback that her husband would even consider such a notion.

Unruffled, Scott said, "Well, I'm going to call the agent and see what he says."

With that, he went into the living room, presumably to call about the house, leaving Ellen alone in the kitchen to finish with the groceries.

Chapter 4

Three days later, Scott and Ellen stood outside 621 Owl Creek Drive. The real estate agent, Jeffrey Slater, had yet to arrive, giving Scott and Ellen a chance to survey the house and its surrounding property. From the outside, the house certainly didn't appear to be in a state of disrepair. Sure, there were a few shingles broken on the slate roof, one of the shutters had come loose on the big, bay window, and the shrubs around the house were a bit overgrown, but overall, the house was in good shape.

While Scott examined the shutter, Ellen wandered around to the back of the house, consumed by the beauty of her surroundings. The house, situated on 2.2 acres was surrounded by woodland, owned by a wealthy investment broker, which Scott had learned from the real estate agent during their telephone conversation. Apparently, the man owned over fifty acres, most of it to the left and back of the property.

To the right of the property was a lake, quiet and calm now, reflecting the late afternoon sunlight off its placid surface. The lake could present a problem with Natalie. She would have to discuss this with Scott, as the last thing she wanted was Natalie falling in and drowning. The thought sent shudders through her body.

Across the lake and through the trees
with their springtime buds, Ellen could make
out the roofline of another house. Other than
that, no other houses could be seen from the rear
of the property. There was a small outbuilding,
perhaps used for storing gardening equipment at
the far end of the yard. Ellen was just about to
have a peek inside when she heard Scott calling
her name from the front of the house.

She momentarily abandoned her
exploration of the property and ran to meet
Scott. As she rounded the side of the house, she
saw that the real estate agent had finally arrived,
his black SUV parked in the driveway. She
joined Scott and the agent on the porch.

"Ah, you must be Mrs. Christianson.
I'm Jeffrey Slater, but you can call me Jeff. I
was just explaining to your husband that this
lock is a little tricky, but I think I can get it open
if you just give me a second." He explained as
he turned the key, pulling the door towards him
at the same time. There was an audible click as
the key engaged the lock and the doorknob
turned. Jeff stood back, indicating they should
go ahead of him.

The first thing Ellen noticed once inside
was the house was very outdated. A green shag
carpet, badly worn and dirty, covered the floor
in the entry and continued down the hall and off
to the right into, what Ellen assumed, was the

living room. A stairwell directly off the entry led upstairs, its banister scratched and lusterless. The walls were painted off-white, but time had taken its toll, leaving them tinged with dirty handprints and scuffmarks.

"As you can see the house needs a bit of work. The previous owners were elderly and let the house deteriorate. Mostly, it just needs a little paint and, oh, yes, there are hardwood floors under this hideous carpet. I'm sure you could refinish them, and they would look beautiful." Jeff explained.

"You said the previous owners were elderly. Are they…" Ellen began.

"Deceased. Yes. Both of them died in a rather tragic accident last fall. Apparently, carbon monoxide poisoning while they were sleeping." Jeff said.

"You mean, they died in this house? That's awful." Ellen said, doubt about the house looming its ugly head in her mind. How could she live in a house knowing two people had perished there?

"Yes, it is awful, but that's partly why the house is such a bargain. That and the couple's son just wants to wash his hands of the whole thing. He inherited the house after their deaths, but already owns a house in Beavercreek. He really doesn't want to deal with paying property taxes on a vacant house and has no interest in moving here to live in it himself, so he hired me to sell it for him." Jeff told them.

"So, is the furnace gas or electric?" Scott asked, clearly trying to change the subject.

"Gas, actually. Unfortunately, the furnace is almost as old as the house, but I'm told it still works well. Hopefully, that won't put you off. This house really has a lot of potential. Why don't you finish looking around? I'll just hang out down here until you're finished. Then, if you have any questions, I'll be happy to answer them." Jeff said.

Ellen and Scott nodded their agreement and headed up the stairs. At the top of the stairs was a long hall with five doors, all of which were shut. Ellen noticed that it was very chilly upstairs, despite the surprisingly warm day they were having. She hung back, rubbing her hands to warm them and surveying the woodwork and walls in the hall, while Scott opened the first door and stepped inside. Ellen could tell that all the woodwork was original and had, apparently never been painted, although it was in need of a fresh coat of varnish. Other than that, it was actually quite beautiful, the wood a deep walnut color.

"Ellen, come check it out." Scott called from within the first room.

Ellen walked through the open door and took in her surroundings. Clearly, this was a bedroom, and had, perhaps, once been a little girl's room, the walls a soft, pink color. The floors in this room were bare, the finish scratched and worn away from years of use. A closet was in the corner and two large windows overlooked the front yard, the view partially obscured by a big oak tree, its branches just beginning to develop green buds.

"Come on, Ell, let's finish looking at the other rooms." Scott said excitedly.

She followed him from the room and down the hall. There were three other bedrooms, all of them quite large. A bathroom, the tiles around the tub dirty with mildew and mold, completed the second-floor layout.

"That's disgusting." Ellen said, indicating the dirty toilet bowl.

"Oh, we can clean that up in no time. The color scheme's not bad; green and white. We can make that work. It's better than the pink in our apartment." Scott told her.

"Yeah. I guess you're right." Ellen said, a bit distracted. Perhaps it was being in a strange house, but she felt odd. It was so cold in the house and a little creepy. When they had been viewing the master bedroom, she had the strange sensation of being watched. She told Scott as much.

"You're just freaked out cause Jeff told you those old people died here. People die in houses all the time, Ellen. It's not a big deal. Someone may have died in our apartment, but it doesn't bother you cause you don't know about it. Now, let's go downstairs and see the kitchen." Scott suggested.

Together, they descended the stairs, the old wood creaking beneath their feet. Jeff was waiting for them downstairs. He led them into the living room which was quite expansive and had a stone fireplace with an intricate carving. Jeff explained that the fireplace was original to the house and actually worked. Large, picture windows overlooked the front and side yard, providing an exquisite view of the lake and surrounding woods.

Next, they viewed the dining room, a large crystal chandelier hanging from the ceiling. The small dining table in their apartment would be dwarfed in a room this size. They would have to invest in a larger table, Ellen decided.

Around the corner from the dining room was the kitchen, the cabinets white, the walls yellow and cheery. The appliances were old and well used, but all of them were rumored to still work and were included with the house. The room made Ellen feel happy, sunlight streaming in from the window above the sink, a

gauzy white sheer curtain gently blowing
from the breeze coming through the partially
open window. Her spirits about the house
suddenly lifted, she asked about the door at the
other end of the kitchen.

"Oh, that's the cellar. I have to tell you,
it's a bit musty down there, but you're free to
take a look." Jeff told them.

Scott looked at Ellen and she shrugged
her shoulders. He took that to mean she was
okay with going into the basement, so, together
they made their way down the stairs, careful to
watch their step in the dim lighting.

Emerging into the main part of the
cellar, they could see a washer and dryer, dusty
and unused, and an old, steel washtub nestled
against the far wall. The rest of the area was
unfurnished, but for an antique looking chair
with a torn upholstered seat sitting against the
wall closest to the stairs. Off the main part of
the cellar was another room, which contained
the furnace, an ancient looking beast, and a hot
water heater that had seen better days. The fuse
box was almost hidden behind the furnace and
Scott said the electric in the house would
eventually have to be updated.

While Scott looked the furnace over,
Ellen wandered back into the main part of the
cellar. She spotted what appeared to be another
door partially obscured by a large mirror leaning

against the wall. As far as she could tell, it didn't lead outside, so maybe it was a closet or another room. Before she could investigate, her thoughts were interrupted by Jeff calling from upstairs.

"Are you guys finished down there? Perhaps you'd like to check out the yard." Jeff shouted down to them.

Scott came out of the furnace room, and they walked back upstairs, joining Jeff in the kitchen.

"So, what do you think? Do you like it? Would you like to put in an offer? If so, I have the paperwork in my car." Jeff eagerly told them.

"I don't know." Ellen said. "We'll have to think about it. The house needs a lot of work and we'll have to invest a lot of money for repairs."

"That's true, but it really is a diamond in the rough, if you ask me. I don't think a house like this is going to stay on the market for long." Jeff prompted. "As a matter-of-fact, I just got a phone call from another agent whose client is very interested in making an offer on the house."

Ellen looked at Scott. She could tell he wanted the house. Hell, what wasn't to want, but she wasn't sure if they should rush into anything. She waited for Scott to say something, but he just stood there, clearly wanting her to make the decision, as if his mind was already made up.

"Could you give us a moment?" she asked Jeff.

"Sure. I'll just run outside to my car. I have a few phone calls to make anyway." He said and headed down the hall towards the door.

"So, what do you want to do?" Scott asked.

"I don't know, Scott. I mean, the house is really big and it's in a good neighborhood, but are we really ready for this?" she asked.

"I think we are. We've been talking about it for a while now and this house seems perfect for us, don't you think? Also, Natalie will love it. I can build her a tree house in that big walnut tree in the backyard. We won't have to worry about her going to a bad school. I think it could really work out." Scott said, his voice giddy with excitement.

Ellen thought it over. Everything Scott said was true. The house was perfect, and Natalie would love it. Still, there was something about the house that gave her pause, something she couldn't put her finger on. In the end, she knew the right thing to do was buy the house and overlook that nagging hesitation she felt. After all, she was certain most first-time homebuyers felt uncertain and more than a little hesitant.

"Okay." She said. "Let's put in an offer."

Chapter 5

"No, Scott, those boxes need to go upstairs." Ellen told her husband, indicating the boxes he was about to place in the living room. It was Friday evening, a little over a month later, and they were spending the weekend moving into their new house.

"I thought you told me these boxes go in here and those boxes by the door go upstairs." Scott said.

"Honey, the boxes are all color coded. The ones you're holding have a green sticker. That means they go in the bathroom upstairs." She told him, as she kissed him on the cheek.

He groaned and started up the stairs with the boxes. "I'm sorry, but I don't understand this color-coding system of yours. Why couldn't you just write 'bathroom' on the box?"

"Well, that would be too easy, wouldn't it?" she said jokingly.

"Mommy, which room is mine again?" Natalie asked from the doorway.

"The one with the pink walls. Go upstairs with Scott and he'll show you." Ellen answered her daughter, absentmindedly rifling through a box of cleaning products in search of the Windex. The mirror above the fireplace had smudges all over it

Suddenly, the old phone on the kitchen wall began to ring. Setting the box aside, Ellen jumped up to answer it.

"Hello." She said into the receiver. Silence greeted her on the other end. Puzzled, she hung up. *Odd.* She thought. She hadn't called the phone company to establish service yet. In fact, she and Scott weren't sure they needed a home line since they both had cell phones.

She picked the receiver up again. Nothing. No dial tone.

Scott came back downstairs at that moment, asking, "Who was on the phone?"

"I don't know. Must be a malfunction in the phone lines. Did you finish putting those boxes away in the bathroom?" she asked

"I sure did. And I gave Natalie the grand tour of her new room. She's busy hanging Winnie the Pooh posters above her bed. I think she's really happy, don't you?" he asked, coming over and pulling her into his arms.

"Yeah. You were right. This was the right thing to do. It's just happened so fast, I still haven't had time to really digest it all, you know?" Ellen replied, nuzzling Scott's neck with her mouth.

"Hmmm. Wanna sneak upstairs for a minute…or several minutes?" he asked with a devilish smile on his face.

Ellen giggled and playfully pushed him away.

"Playing hard to get, huh? I get it. We'll rendezvous later when everything is in order. Right now, let's finish getting unpacked. Then, I'm going to whip up my famous spaghetti and meatballs. How's that sound?"

"I don't know how famous it is, but it sounds great. I'm famished." Ellen said, heading outside to get the rest of the boxes out of the moving truck.

....

Later that evening, after dinner, while Scott read Natalie a bedtime story, Ellen had just finished washing the dinner dishes and putting them away. She sat down at the small kitchen table to reflect on the day's events.

They had somehow managed to get most of the boxes unpacked and put away. She noticed, however, that the furniture they had in their apartment, which once seemed comfortable and cozy, now seemed inadequate and sparse in such a big home. Perhaps in a few months, they could purchase some new items. Ellen pondered over what she would like to buy if they had the money. Definitely a new sofa, their current one a hand-me-down from Scott's parents that had certainly seen better days.

Also, she had always wanted a china hutch for her dining room so that she could adorn its shelves with the blue and white china, the only thing remaining of her mother's, she loved so much.

As Ellen sat, lost in thought, dreaming of beautiful antiques and expensive rugs, the door to the basement suddenly came ajar. The sound of its creaking hinges awoke Ellen from her dreamy trance. She looked up and watched as the door continued to swing open slowly, as though someone were giving it a gentle push.

Getting up, she walked over to the door, feeling a faint sense of panic creep over her. *What if someone was in the basement?* She wondered. As Ellen looked, it was obvious no one was standing on the other side, the basement stairwell empty, save for a few dust bunnies. Standing there, Ellen tested the door, and chided herself for being so paranoid. It swung easily on its hinges and as she closed it, she heard the knob catch in the frame. She pulled it towards her just to be sure it was shut. Satisfied, she returned to the table.

No sooner had she sat down, than the door swung open again, this time much more quickly, hitting the kitchen wall with a bang. The sound startled Ellen and she jumped up, racing down the hall and yelling for Scott.

"What's the matter?" he asked, rapidly descending the stairs, concern clouding his face.

"The basement door…came open…I think someone's down there." Ellen stammered, clearly alarmed.

Scott, sensing his wife's anxiety, grabbed a poker from the fireplace and headed towards the kitchen, Ellen following closely behind.

"Scott, what are you going to do?" she demanded, frightened for his safety.

He didn't answer her, but instead stealthily crept across the kitchen floor, poker in hand, ready to swing at any moment.

Ellen snatched up her cell phone, prepared to dial 911 if there was any sign of a threat to Scott's wellbeing. She watched as Scott descended the basement stairs, slowly and expertly, searching for a possible assailant. Moments passed, seeming more like an eternity to Ellen.

Finally, Scott emerged from the basement, holding a thin and rather mangy looking kitten in his arms.

"I found your intruder." He said. "We're lucky the little guy didn't make off with your jewelry before we caught him."

Clearly, he was making a joke, but Ellen didn't find it all that funny. She had been genuinely frightened and didn't approve of being poked fun at.

"Ha, ha, very funny. How did a kitten get in the basement?" Ellen wanted to know, her frayed nerves finally calming down at the sight of the frail feline.

"I don't know. He must have wandered in somehow. He looks hungry. Do we have any milk?" he asked, opening the refrigerator.

"I heard you're not supposed to give cats milk. I think it gives them diarrhea." Ellen replied, not sure where she had heard this information.

"Well, we need to feed him something. The little guy's starving. Who knows how long he's been trapped in that basement." Scott said, rummaging around with his free hand in search of a meal for the kitten.

Eventually, he came across a can of tuna and, as Ellen watched, he opened the can and sat it down on the floor, showing it to the kitten, who immediately began to devour the fish as though it were his first meal in days.

"Look, I told you he was hungry." Scott pointed out.

Ellen didn't say anything, but, rather, watched the little kitten eat, its belly slowly expanding, growing round and full. She had to admit the fuzzy little cat was kind of cute, despite its black fur being caked with mud and some other unidentifiable substance.

Around that time, Natalie had come downstairs to see what all the commotion was about. Her eyes, already big and round, suddenly grew enormous, excitement filling them like a giant balloon.

"Mommy is that a kitten?" she asked, knowing full well that it was, but not understanding why it was in their kitchen.

"Yes, sweetie. We found him in the basement." Ellen told her, smiling at her daughter's delightful innocence.

"Are we going to keep him?" Natalie wanted to know, running over to the kitten and scooping him up in her tiny little arms. Immediately, he began to purr and rub his face against hers.

"I don't know, Nat. We'll have to see if he belongs to anyone first." Ellen said, trying to be reasonable.

"Okay, but if he doesn't belong to anybody, then can we keep him?" Natalie asked, a pleading tone in her voice.

"We'll see." Ellen said, already knowing what the outcome would be.

"Can he sleep in my bed tonight?" Natalie asked.

"I don't see a problem with that." Scott said, looking at his wife for confirmation.

Ellen nodded her head and watched as Natalie joyfully sauntered down the hall and up the stairs, the tiny kitten clutched closely to her chest.

Chapter 6

As it turned out, the kitten was homeless as Ellen discovered after a thorough canvas of the neighborhood. How he had gotten into their basement would forever remain a mystery, but he was now, officially, their cat. They named him Boo, which Scott found appropriate given Ellen's state of fright when he made his existence known. Natalie agreed the name suited him and laughed every time Scott held the kitten out to Ellen and said 'boo'.

Ellen took him to the vet for all his necessary vaccinations and to be neutered, and then made a trip, along with Natalie, to the local pet supply store where they purchased food, toys, and litter box necessities.

Ellen set his litter box up in the basement where she felt it would be less conspicuous if they had guests over. As it turned out, Boo had been using the whole basement as his personal litter box during his imprisonment, so Ellen spent the better part of two hours scrubbing the floor with bleach and special pet odor formula to remove the smell of urine. Despite all this, she really took a shine to the cat, who, in turn took a shine to her, often coming downstairs to keep her company after everyone else was asleep.

They left the basement door ajar so that Boo could go downstairs to do his business. Often, Ellen would find herself staring at the door, wondering how the little kitten had pushed it open that night. Occasionally, when no one else was around, she would place Boo on the top basement step, close the door, and wait to see if he could open it. Each time, though, Boo would simply meow from the other side of the door and stick one of his velvety black paws underneath, as if to remind her that she had forgotten him.

Ellen tried to forget about that night's strange events, but despite her best efforts, she remained convinced that the cat had not been the culprit for opening the door. Yet, as the weeks passed, no other incidents took place, and Ellen became certain that the whole thing would remain a mystery. She began to forget about the occurrence and fell into a daily routine of taking Natalie to daycare and herself to work. In the evenings, she and Scott would take turns preparing dinner, washing dishes, and doing laundry.

One evening, while Ellen was in the basement, sorting through the dirty clothes, she began to feel uneasy. She couldn't figure out what the source of her distress was, but, after a while, it became almost overwhelming. She was just about at the point of giving up on the laundry and retreating upstairs when the light in the basement went out, leaving her in utter, complete darkness.

For a moment, she stood there, a pair of Scott's dirty boxers in her hand, unable to move. After a while, she began fiddling with the light bulb above the laundry tub, twisting it back and forth in an attempt to turn the light back on. Her efforts were fruitless, and she was just about to feel her way upstairs in search of a new light bulb when she felt the unmistakable sensation of breathing on the back of her neck. There was no sound, only the steady, warm whisper of breath on her skin. Momentarily, her heart stopped beating as fear raced through her veins, freezing her limbs and rendering them useless.

Suddenly, the light in the basement flickered back on. Ellen, regaining control of her legs, took off running up the stairs. She never looked back for she was certain that, if she had, someone or something would have been standing there.

Once upstairs, she ran to find Scott, who was watching television in the living room with Natalie.

"Scott, can I speak with you in the kitchen, please?" she asked, her voice wavering slightly.

"Okay, hon." He said, as he pried himself up off the sofa and moved towards the kitchen.

In the bright light of the kitchen, Scott could see that his wife looked very pale and shaken. Tentatively, he asked, "What's wrong?"

"Scott," she began, "someone was in the basement with me. I know it sounds crazy, but I was doing laundry, then the light went out, and I felt someone breathing on my neck. I was so scared. I couldn't move." She knew she was rambling but couldn't control herself.

"Sweetheart, calm down. Here, why don't you have a seat?" he asked, pulling out a chair for her.

Sinking into the chair, Ellen took a deep breath and again tried to explain what had just happened to her. She told Scott the whole story from the beginning, certain not to leave any details out. After she had finished speaking, she sat there, staring at him expectantly.

At first, Scott said nothing, the wheels in his mind turning, obviously trying to come up with a plausible explanation for his wife's strange story.

Finally, he told her he would go have a look in the basement. She tried to stop him, not wanting him to experience anything like she had felt, but he insisted, so she let him go.

After a while, Scott returned, and reported nothing amiss in the basement. He explained that he checked the whole area from top to bottom, but there simply wasn't anyone or anything down there. Ellen tried to argue with him, insisting that she had felt someone, but her protests were futile, as there was no proof to support her claims. Eventually, she gave up and went to bed, where she laid awake tossing and turning, unable to forget the unpleasant sensation she had felt.

Chapter 7

From that point forward, Ellen was afraid to go into the basement. She knew it was irrational, but she made excuses for her unwillingness to travel downstairs. She even went so far as to tell Scott that she had seen a rat, which he knew she was mortified of, so that he would do the laundry instead of her. Naturally, he also assumed the role of cleaning the litter box, which still remained in the basement.

Ellen wasn't sure if Scott bought into her pretenses. She suspected that he knew the real reason she would no longer venture into the basement, but he went along with her stories of rats and sprained ankles, perhaps, just to placate her until she came to her senses. Either way, Ellen was more than happy to let him do the laundry and clean the litter box. In exchange, she did all the housecleaning and washed the dishes. They still took turns cooking, though, and one evening, while Scott was busily preparing meatloaf, Ellen decided to take a walk.

By this time, it was mid-May. They had lived in their new house for nearly two months, and spring was slowly giving way to summer. All the trees were in full bloom and the evenings balmy and pleasant, the air filled with the sweet nectarous scent of honeysuckle.

After locating her gym shoes, Ellen set out on her evening saunter down Owl Creek Drive. It was just after 6:00pm and still light out, affording Ellen the opportunity to view the gorgeous countryside dappled, occasionally, with a house or two.

Actually, there were only five houses on her street, most of which were set back a considerable distance from the road. Her own home had the smallest lot with most homes on the street consisting of ten or more acres. She had learned, during the closing for her home that it originally sat on seventeen acres but much of the land had been sold years before to the investment banker that lived behind Ellen.

Ellen had just reached the end of Owl Creek Drive and decided to turn around and head back when she spotted an elderly couple turning the corner off of Western Avenue. The man had silver hair, deep-set eyes, and carried most of his weight around the belly. The woman, presumably his wife, had short-cropped reddish hair, sprinkled with flecks of silver. They both were dressed in shorts, polo style shirts, and tennis shoes.

"Hello." The man said, coming up to Ellen. "You must be who bought the Garritson's house. I'm Stanley Fischer and this

is my wife, Noreen. We live at the end of
Owl Creek just past the bend."

"My name's Ellen Christianson and, yes,
my husband and I did buy the Garritson's house.
It's a pleasure to meet you." Ellen said,
extending her hand to shake.

"It's a shame what happened to them,
the Garritson's, I mean." Noreen stated, clearly
looking to gossip.

Ellen took the bait, "Yes. It's a tragedy.
I understand they died from carbon monoxide
poisoning, but I never got the whole story."

"Ah, the medical examiner ruled it
accidental. Henry was getting on in the years
and wasn't very good about maintaining things
around the house. Apparently, the pipe leading
to the flue on the furnace was broken, rusted and
worn. Henry and Gale never had a clue, died in
their sleep one night. Their housecleaner found
them a few days later. It was just awful. They
were really nice people." Stanley explained.

"It wasn't an accident." Noreen
interjected.

"Excuse me?" Ellen inquired.

"Don't listen to her. She watches too
many of those forensic shows. She thinks
everyone who dies was murdered." Stanley
concluded gruffly.

"No, I don't, Stanley. But Gale told me strange things had been happening in the house for a while." Noreen said.

"What kinds of strange things?" Ellen wanted to know.

"You know noises and doors opening, things like that. She was really scared." She said.

"Hogwash!" Stanley retorted. "Gale was as crazy as you."

"Stanley, you shouldn't talk about the dead that way. It's disrespectful. Besides, I believed her." Noreen explained.

"How long did this go on?" Ellen wanted to know.

"Gale told me it had been going on for years. It would stop for a while, and then start again out of the blue. If you ask me, someone killed them. In fact, I think it was that snake-in-the-grass, Jack Winters." Noreen said, referring to the investment banker that lived behind Ellen.

"This is news to me. Why on earth would Jack want to kill Henry and Gale?" Stanley demanded.

"Stanley, you are so close-minded." Noreen said, turning back to Ellen. "Jack wants to own all the property in this area so that he can build a mall. He already bought most of the land that went with your house years ago, but Henry and Gale refused to sell the rest. He was trying to force them to sell by scaring them. When that didn't work, he murdered them."

"Well, then why didn't he buy the property once he whacked them, and they were out of the picture?" Stanley asked.

"Obviously, Ellen and her husband beat him to the punch." Noreen said, satisfied that she had solved all aspects of the crime.

Ellen doubted this was the case, given the house had been on the market for over two months before she and Scott put in an offer. If Jack Winters had killed the Garritson's so that he could buy their house, he certainly would've done it before Ellen and Scott bought it. She kept this information to herself, however, not wanting to rain on Noreen's crime-solving parade.

By this time, it was getting late. Ellen explained to the Fischers that she had to get home and help with dinner. They said their good-byes and Ellen made a beeline home, mulling over her conversation with Noreen and Stan along the way.

After dinner, Ellen relayed her conversation with the Fischers to Scott.

"They sound kooky." He said absently, as he polished off his second bowl of ice cream.

"They were a little odd, I guess, but I liked them. By the way, if you keep eating like

that, you're going to lose your manly figure."
Ellen told him, a hint of a smile on her lips.

"Oh, really? Tell me this: will you still
love me when I'm old, fat and bald?" he asked,
pulling her down beside him.

"I don't know, honey. There are plenty
of other fish in the sea." She said trying to
maintain a straight face.

"Ah, but can they do this?" he asked,
kissing her fully and deeply on the mouth.

Later that night, Ellen lay in bed, fully
awake and restless, her mind trying to make a
connection between the odd events she had
experienced and the strange happenings that had
occurred with the Garritson's. She wondered if
their deaths had really been an accident or was
Noreen right about them being murdered. Yet,
that didn't really make sense to her, either.
After all, if someone had killed them, how did
that explain what was happening to her?

Scott lay next to her, his deep, even
breathing an indication that he was asleep.

As she continued to lie there, her mind
wandered back to the night in the basement,
when she had the strange sense of someone
breathing on her neck. Clearly, if someone had
been in the basement with her that night, Scott
would have found him or her. So, what had
caused her to feel so uneasy? Had she imagined
the whole thing? Could it have been a breeze

coming through a crack in the window?
These questions continued to plague her until,
finally, she fell into a fitful sleep.

Chapter 8

The lake was glistening in the mid-afternoon sunlight. Ellen sat on the bank, reading a romance novel, the sun's warm rays dancing on her skin. She was engrossed in her book, unaware of her surroundings, allowing the day to drift away page by page.

After a while, Ellen had the strange sensation that someone was watching her. She glanced up from her book and looked around. On the other side of the lake, standing on the edge of the bank, was a young girl. She had long, golden hair that hung forward, partially obscuring her face. She was dressed in jeans and a white peasant blouse. She appeared to be deep in thought and unaware that Ellen was watching her.

Ellen was just about to call out to the girl when, for no apparent reason, the girl flung herself into the lake. Momentarily stunned, Ellen just sat there staring at the spot the girl had dived into. Several seconds passed, but the girl did not resurface. Alarmed, Ellen stood up and ran to the other side of the lake, peering into its eerily calm surface. She couldn't see the girl, as the water was slightly murky and cast green from algae. As she continued to let her eyes search the water, looking for some sign of the girl, she spotted the faint outline of

*something floating up towards the surface.
Aghast, Ellen stumbled backwards as the girl's
lifeless body reached the surface, her face
down, arms and legs hanging limply in the
water.*

*After a few moments passed, Ellen crept
to the edge of the lake and gently reached out
towards the girl. She knew she had to try to
revive her. Although she had never learned
CPR, she had seen it performed on television
several times, and felt she had to at least try.*

*As Ellen began to pull the girl's body
towards the bank, the girl suddenly grabbed
Ellen's outstretched arm. Ellen lost her balance
and tumbled headfirst into the lake, the inky
dark water swallowing her body completely.
Confused and disoriented, she frantically
clawed through the water, trying to reach the
surface, her lungs already burning from lack of
oxygen.*

*Just as her head broke the surface,
something pulled her back down. Ellen
struggled against whatever held her, but she
was losing the battle, as her body was pulled
further and further down towards the bottom of
the lake. Helplessly, she watched as the light
from the surface began to fade away, leaving
her in near pitch-blackness.*

*As she hit the lake's bottom, panic seized
her body as her lungs cried out for precious*

*oxygen. Ellen tried to see what was holding
her, preventing her from swimming to the
surface. Though it was very dark, enough light
reached the bottom of the lake to allow Ellen to
see that it was the girl that was grasping her
ankle, her face still hidden behind her hair.
Ellen tried to push the girl off of her, but the
girl's grip was strong, leaving Ellen exhausted
from the exertion.*

*Without warning, the girl released her
grasp and Ellen watched in dismay as the skin
on the girl's hands began to fall off, leaving the
bare bone exposed. Then, the girl's hair floated
away from her face, revealing her scull, the face
locked in a permanent expression of horror.*

Ellen woke from the dream with a start,
her body drenched in sweat and every nerve in
her body tingling with fear. Glancing at the
alarm clock on the nightstand, she saw that it
was just after 3:00 am. Scott lay beside her,
apparently undisturbed by his wife's nightmare.

Unable to fall back asleep, Ellen pushed
the tangled blankets aside and got out of bed,
feeling her way in the darkness down the hall to
the bathroom. She washed her face and used the
toilet, then headed downstairs to the kitchen,
careful to be quiet so as not to wake Natalie.

After pouring herself a glass of juice,
Ellen slumped down at the kitchen table. She
sipped the juice slowly, while her mind

pondered the dream she had had. She had never been prone to nightmares, though she had to admit she did have a vivid imagination. What would have prompted her to have such a dream though? She hadn't watched any scary movies lately. Perhaps the dream had resulted from her strange conversation with the Fischers.

As she continued to wonder over the nature of her dream, Boo sauntered into the kitchen, meowing softly as he jumped into her lap. Smiling, she began to stroke the back of his head and scratch behind his ears, just the way he liked. He rewarded her with loud purring and began kneading her legs.

Just as she had made up her mind to return to bed, Boo suddenly jumped off her lap. He ran halfway across the kitchen, the hair on his back standing straight up and stared at the cracked basement door. A low, guttural growl erupted from the back of his throat, as he laid his ears flat against the top of his head.

"What's wrong, Boo?" Ellen asked the cat. She had never seen him act this way before.

Boo continued to stare at the door, intermittently hissing and growling, ignoring Ellen as she crouched beside him and attempted to comfort him.

Abruptly, the basement door was flung open, startling Boo and causing him to go streaking down the hall into the living room, leaving Ellen alone in the kitchen. Her heart racing, Ellen was about to dart down the hall behind Boo when she saw a hazy white glow materialize in front of the open basement door.

Transfixed, Ellen stood there watching, as the hazy white glow lingered in the doorway. Although the urge to flee was overwhelming, Ellen was unable to move her feet. It was if some invisible force held her there. She continued to watch as the hazy glow began to fade, and then totally disappeared before her eyes.

Confused and unsure of what she had seen, Ellen took a few deep breaths to calm herself. Despite her fear, she was surprised with herself for not running. Maybe she was just tired of being afraid and needed, for the sake of her own sanity, to prove, once and for all, that no one was hiding in the basement. Whatever the reason, Ellen found herself moving in the direction of the basement, her stride slow and deliberate.

Upon reaching the top of the stairs, she could see the stairwell was empty. Flipping on the light, she began to descend the stairs, her heart thumping heavily against her ribcage. Halfway down, she stopped and listened, prepared to flee to the safety of the kitchen at the slightest sound. Yet, the basement remained reassuringly quiet. Ellen swallowed hard and walked down the remaining few steps.

Uncertain of what she was looking for or what she would do if she found it, Ellen began searching the main part of the basement for any clue to what was going on. She looked behind the washer and dryer and then the laundry tub. There didn't appear to be anything out of place as far as she could tell, although she did notice a stray sock, partially hidden under the back corner of the washer.

Next, she moved into the furnace room. She checked all around the hot water heater and furnace, casting aside spider webs and dust bunnies, but saw nothing that offered an explanation for the strange happenings in the house. Sighing loudly, she moved back into the main room and surveyed her surroundings.

Just as she was beginning to think this was a crazy idea, she spotted the closed door with the mirror leaning against it. She and Scott had opened the door after moving in and had discovered it was an old, empty coal room. The area wasn't insulated and, apparently leaked whenever it rained. As a result, it was rather dank and dirty with dark spots of mold covering the walls. Having recently watched a particularly disturbing Dateline Special she had been concerned that Natalie might get sick from the mold, so she had Scott put a combination lock on the door and hadn't opened the door since.

Standing in front of the door, she tried to recall the combination. She was certain they had agreed to use Natalie's birth date, so she tried those numbers: 8-26-16. She was rewarded with a click as the lock unsnapped. Carefully, she moved the mirror aside and pulled the door open, its rusty hinges resisting at first.

Once the door was open, Ellen suddenly remembered there was no light in the room. She quickly located a flashlight kept on the shelf above the washer and returned to the room, flicking the flashlight on as she walked through the doorway.

The first thing Ellen noticed was that the room was considerably cooler than the rest of the basement. Her fear returned at that moment, as the room was so dark and reminded her of some sort of torture chamber. She tried to push the image out of her mind as she ran the beam from the flashlight over the walls and floor of the room. The walls were constructed from stone blocks and the floor was concrete. She could see there was water collected in a small puddle in the far right corner, probably a result of the rainstorm from a few nights before.

Just as she was about to turn and leave, she noticed the mortar around one of the blocks was missing. Carefully, she knelt down and pushed on the block. At first, it remained solid, but as she persisted, it eventually began to move a little. Laying the flashlight on the floor to free up her other hand, she wedged her fingers in the gap around the block and began moving it back and forth. Slowly, she began to wriggle the block out, her fingers aching from the jagged edges of the stone.

Once the block was completely free, she picked the flashlight up and shone its beam into the crevice. The hole went a good ways back, and Ellen struggled to see anything. The beam from the flashlight was weak, so it took her a few moments to spot the outline of a small, metal box shoved into the very back of the cavity. She reached her entire arm into the opening, straining a great effort to reach the box. Finally, her fingers grasped the handle on the box and she pulled it out.

Carrying the box into the next room, she placed it on top of the dryer. Thankfully, there was no lock, and she was able to open the box without difficulty. Inside was a single gold chain with a locket attached. Ellen picked up the locket and turned it over, revealing a faint engraving on the back: *Love, Mom.* Opening the locket exposed a blurry photo of a smiling teenage girl with golden hair and green eyes.

Odd, Ellen thought. Why did someone go to the trouble of hiding this?

Unable to answer that question at the moment and exhausted from all her efforts, Ellen returned to the coal room, replaced the block, and shut the door and locked it. Then, with the metal box and locket in tow, she made her way back upstairs. Placing the box in a kitchen cabinet, she returned to bed, where she fell into a deep, undisturbed sleep.

Chapter 9

The next afternoon Ellen left work early, feigning stomach cramps, and made a beeline for the public library. She had yet to visit this particular library so it took her a while to find what she was looking for. With the assistance of a pretty, young librarian, she located a computer and logged in using the ID number on her library card. She really wasn't sure what she was looking for, but she decided to try to find some articles on the history of her house.

After twenty minutes of searching, she finally discovered an article dated back nearly twenty years. She began to read the article.

Tragedy struck a local family yesterday afternoon when the body of missing girl, Emily Garritson, was found in a ditch along Rt. 42 just outside of Crescentville. A road clean-up crew discovered the body around 3:00 PM.

The girl had been missing for nearly three days, disappearing after school on Friday following a football game. When she didn't return home by curfew, her parents, Henry and Gale Garritson, called the authorities to report their daughter missing.

"This just isn't like Emily. She would never stay out and not call us." Said a very distraught Gale Garritson during an exclusive interview with Crescentville Chronicle's

*reporter, Abigail Freeman the day after the
reported disappearance.*

*Over the following days, a countywide
search ensued, but turned up nothing. The
police interviewed several friends and family
members, including Emily's boyfriend, Toby
Price. "I don't know where Emily is", Price
said during an emotional televised interview, "If
I did, I would definitely tell."*

*The police are refusing comment at this
time, but are scheduled to hold a news
conference tomorrow morning.*

*A memorial is being held for Emily
outside her school, Crescentville High, at 7:00
PM this evening. People are asked to attend
and offer support for her family and friends.*

A black and white photo of a smiling
Emily Garritson accompanied the article. The
picture, taken earlier that year, revealed an
attractive dark-haired girl with blue eyes and
freckles. Ellen read the article several times
before continuing her search. Two days later,
she found another article pertaining to Emily
Garritson.

*Police were astonished to find the body
of Morton Sullivan in his home early this
morning. According to sources, Sullivan, age
thirty-seven, shot himself sometime late last
night. The police arrived at his home to arrest*

him in connection to the strangulation of local girl, Emily Garritson.

"We're certain Sullivan was behind the death of Emily Garritson", said Detective Ronald Crawley, "He had several items belonging to Miss Garritson in his possession, including her book bag and a sweater she was wearing the night of her disappearance."

Sources say that Sullivan, a convicted sexual predator, was interviewed several times by police prior to his apparent suicide.

"It's police protocol to interview all known sex offenders whenever a crime is committed." Said Police Chief, Robert Belmont. Though Emily was not sexually assaulted, police believe there was a sexual component to her murder.

Emily Garritson's parents expressed relief that Sullivan was dead during an interview with our very own, Abigail Freeman. "We just want to put this whole thing behind us. It has destroyed our family." Said Henry Garritson.

The funeral of Emily Garritson is scheduled to be held at Baumert and Klein funeral home Friday morning at 10:00 AM.

There were several more articles printed at later dates attempting to offer an explanation for Emily Garritson's murder. According to the articles, police strongly felt that Morton

Sullivan had kidnapped Emily, and then murdered her. When the police began asking questions, Sullivan, not wanting to return to prison, shot himself. When the police searched his home, they discovered Emily's book bag and sweater stashed in a trashcan behind his house. Sullivan had previously been convicted of the rape of another girl, Allison Burton. He had served five years of a seven-year sentence in the state penitentiary and was released early for good behavior. He had been living in Crescentville just three months before Emily Garritson was murdered.

Ellen sat back from the microfiche machine, stretching her arms overhead. Glancing at her watch, she saw that she had been sitting at the library for nearly two hours. Her eyes hurt and she had a crick in the neck. Deciding to give up her search for the day, she logged off and headed outside, thanking the librarian on her way out the door.

Later that evening, Ellen sat in the living room, Natalie sleeping on the couch next to her. She held the locket in her hand, staring at it, wondering whom it belonged to and why it was hidden in her basement. After seeing the picture of Emily in the newspaper article, Ellen could rule Emily out as the girl in the locket.

"Whatcha doing?" Scott asked from the doorway.

"Nothing. Just trying to relax." She replied, tucking the locket between the cushions of the couch. She hadn't told Scott about finding it and, for some reason, wasn't ready to tell him just yet. She needed more information before she tried explaining any of this to anyone.

"Long day, huh?" he asked, sitting in the recliner across from her.

"I guess. My neck is killing me." She said, rubbing the back of her neck.

"Listen, my mother called and wants me to come help her clean out the attic this weekend. I thought it would be a great chance for us to get away for a little while. You know they just had a pool installed in their backyard." Scott told her.

Ellen didn't want to go to Scott's parents this weekend. She had plans to try and talk with the Fischers again and see if they knew anything about Emily Garritson. She quickly tried to come up with an excuse to bail out.

"Shoot. My boss asked me to work on Saturday and I told him I would. There's this big case he's working on and needs my help with some of the research. Why don't you and Natalie go without me?" she asked, trying her best to look disappointed.

"Can't you get out of work?" Scott persisted.

"I don't think so, hon. Andrew is working against the clock on this case. He really needs me. You know he hardly ever asks me to work on the weekend." She said, feeling guilty about lying.

Scott looked annoyed for a moment, but then said resignedly, "Okay. I guess it'll just be Natalie and me. She's going to love the pool, don't you think?"

They continued to talk about Natalie, the pool, and other normal topics for an hour or so. It was nice to take her mind off of the mystery surrounding her house, even if it was just temporary.

Before long, Ellen found herself yawning and realized it was getting late. She hadn't slept well the night before and she really needed to get some work done at the office tomorrow since she had skipped out early today. She asked Scott if he would mind putting Natalie to bed and then headed upstairs. She was asleep before her head hit the pillow.

Chapter 10

Two days later, Ellen sat alone in her bedroom. She had already put Natalie to bed and Scott was in Cleveland on an unexpected overnight business trip. She was mulling over the articles she had copied at the library pertaining to Emily Garritson's murder. There had to be something in them that would give her a better idea of what was going on in her house. Surely there was a connection between the strange events in her house and the brutal murder of the young girl who once lived there. Ellen just needed to keep looking. Though she had returned to the library after work the day before, she hadn't turned up anything new.

She had also made a quick stop at the local courthouse and made copies of ownership documents on her house dating back to the time it was built. As it had turned out, there had only been five owners, including herself.

The first owner of the house had been a doctor by the name of Harvey Simmons. He had the house built back in 1911. A widower, he had never remarried and had lived in the house until his death in 1929 after a long battle with cancer.

Next, a couple, David and Sarah Percy, had purchased the house in June of 1929. They were young and had five children. The family had lived in the house for twenty-one years. By this time, their children apparently grown, they sold the house and moved to Florida.

Jonathon and June Morgan had then moved into the house. They only lived there for eight years. As far as Ellen could tell, they had no children, but further research had revealed that they had one child shortly before they sold the house in 1958.

After that, the Garritson's had bought the home. At the time of their deaths, Henry was 72 and Gale was 70, so they would have been quite young when they bought their home. They had adopted their son, Eric, in 1970 when he was just a baby. A little over two years later, Gale became pregnant with Emily.

As far as Ellen could tell, nothing about the previous owners would explain the strange things happening in her home. Not to mention, she had found no evidence of a girl fitting the description of the one in the locket. The photo was too recent to have been one of the Percy clan and the Morgans had a son. So, if she hadn't lived in the house, who was she?

Tired and unsure of her next move, Ellen put the documents away in her desk drawer. She decided there was nothing more she could do tonight. It was getting late and she had to be up early for work.

She needed to use the bathroom, so she headed down the hall. After brushing her teeth and washing her face, Ellen checked on Natalie. The little girl was peacefully sleeping on her side, Boo curled up at her feet. The image brought a smile to Ellen's face.

Returning to her bedroom, Ellen stopped short. On her pillow lay a single sheet of paper. She was certain she had put everything away before her trip to the bathroom. Trepidation filled her, but she forced her legs to walk over to the bed.

There, lying on her pillow was a picture of the Garritson family, taken during happier times. Accompanying the photo was a follow-up article on Emily's murder. Ellen had read the article many times in hopes of discovering something new.

The faces of Henry, Gale, Eric, and Emily lay there staring up at her. How had it gotten on her pillow? She was certain everything had been put away. And besides, she had turned the covers down after she had put the articles in the desk, so how did this one get on her pillow?

Uneasy, Ellen decided to sleep in Natalie's room. She knew if she stayed in her bedroom, she would never fall asleep. So, grabbing her cell phone from the nightstand, Ellen hurriedly left the room.

The rest of the week passed slowly and by the time Scott and Natalie finally left for the weekend, Ellen could barely hold her patience in check. She desperately wanted to talk to the Fischers, but when she knocked on their door Saturday morning, there was no answer. Apparently, they had gone out because their car was not in the driveway. Aggravated, Ellen quickly scrawled a note asking them to call her, and then returned home.

She spent the better part of the afternoon cleaning the house from top to bottom. The work helped keep her mind off the house and Emily Garritson. By the time she had finished scrubbing the bathroom tub, having finally won the battle she had waged with a lime stain, she felt more like herself.

The chirping of her cell phone nearly caused her to fall off the ladder she was using to dust off the ceiling fan blades in the living room.

"Hello." She said.

"Ellen? This is Noreen Fischer. You asked me to call. Is everything alright?" Noreen asked, worry fringing her words.

"Oh, yes. Everything is fine. Thanks for calling. Listen, I wanted to ask you a few questions. Would you like to come over and have some iced tea? It's so nice outside; I

thought we could chat on the back deck."
Ellen said, hoping Noreen wouldn't turn her
down.

"That sounds wonderful. Shall I come
over now?" Noreen asked.

"Um, now is fine. I'm not really doing
anything and would love the company." Ellen
said.

Ellen hung up the phone and waited by
the front door for Noreen to arrive. Although
she was expecting it, the knock on the door
startled her.

"Come in." Ellen told Noreen, smiling
brightly at the other woman.

Ellen busied herself preparing glasses of
iced tea, and then took Noreen out on the back
deck, which overlooked the woods and lake.

"I'm really glad you came over. I've
been meaning to invite you for a while now."
Ellen told the older lady.

"Well, thanks for having me over. By
the way, this tea is heavenly." Noreen said,
taking another sip of her drink.

Ellen wasn't sure how to begin, so she
just plunged right in. "You knew the Garritsons
for a long time, didn't you?"

"Yes. We moved here just six months
after they did. It didn't take long for Gale and
me to hit it off. We had so much in common."
Noreen said fondly.

"I know this sounds a little odd, but I've been researching the history of my house and I learned that the Garritsons had a daughter, Emily, that was killed. Did you know her?" Ellen asked tentatively.

Noreen sat her tea down and stared off into the distance, not answering Ellen right away.

"I'd almost forgotten." Noreen began. "It's been so long since Emily died. Yes, I knew her. She was a wonderful girl. She used to watch our dog for us when we went on vacation. It was a tragedy, what happened to her, I mean."

"How did her parents deal with it?" Ellen asked.

"Henry bottled it up inside, but Gale was a complete wreck. They almost divorced because of it. If it hadn't been for Eric, their son, I think they probably would've." Noreen answered.

"Was Emily's brother with her the night she disappeared?" Ellen wanted to know.

"No. He was a few years older than Emily. I think he was out with friends maybe. I really don't remember. It's been so long." Noreen said.

"Were they close?" Ellen asked.

"Not really. As I said, Eric was older. Also, Eric was different from Emily. He gave

Gale and Henry some problems. You know, always coming home late, hanging around with the wrong crowd, and things like that. Nothing too serious, but Gale and Henry were strict and disapproved of his lifestyle. Emily was always an angel. She got good grades and helped out around the house. Sometimes, I think he resented Emily for being so perfect. When she died, though, he took it really hard. After that, he changed for the better. He went to college and got a good job." Noreen said.

"I met him at the closing for our house. He seemed a little cold and distant." Ellen told Noreen.

"Yes, well, that sounds like Eric. He was never much of a talker. Sort of kept to himself. Introverted is what I think they call it nowadays. He was adopted, you know?" Noreen said.

"Yes. I did a little research on the family and discovered that. Why did they adopt a child?" Ellen asked. "I mean, they had Emily so there really wasn't a need to adopt…"

"Oh, you see, Gale was told she couldn't have children, so they adopted Eric. A couple years later, Gale found out she was pregnant. She thought it was a miracle. Anyway, I think that's why Eric was a little bit of a troublemaker. Maybe he never felt like he belonged." Noreen said.

For a while, the two women lapsed into silence, quietly sipping their tea and enjoying the beautiful day.

Finally, Noreen spoke, "I never really understood how that man got her."

"You mean Emily's murderer?" Ellen asked.

"Yes. She was always so careful. I can't imagine why she would've gone with him." Noreen replied.

"Who knows? Maybe he snuck up on her. Hey, can I show you something?" Ellen asked, withdrawing the locket from her pocket and handing it to Noreen.

Noreen studied the locket for a few moments then asked, "Who is this?"

"I was hoping you could tell me. I found it in my basement. Do you have any idea who the girl is?" Ellen asked hopefully.

"I don't think so. But then again, my memory isn't what it used to be." Noreen said, handing the locket back to Ellen.

They continued to talk for a while longer, but Ellen was unable to learn anything of value that would help her figure out what was going on in her house. Although she felt she could trust Noreen, she was reluctant to share the strange events in her house with the woman.

Eventually, Noreen said she had to be getting home. As Ellen said goodbye, she promised to have Noreen over again. She really did enjoy the older woman's company.

Monday night, Ellen couldn't sleep. She sat at the kitchen table, absently filing her nails and eating a bowl of corn flakes, while her mind wandered over the events of the past few months. *Who was the girl in the locket and did it have anything to do with Emily Garritson's murder?* She wondered. Though she wasn't sure what, she felt she was onto something. Perhaps something that would help explain what was going on in her house. She decided that first thing tomorrow morning, she would try to look up Emily's old boyfriend, Toby Price. Maybe he knew more than he had told the police. At the very least, he might recognize the girl in the locket. It had to be one of Emily's friends, but Ellen couldn't understand why it was hidden in the basement.

Getting up from the table, Ellen took her empty bowl to the sink and began washing it out. As she finished rinsing the bowl, she placed it in the strainer next to the sink. Reaching for a towel to dry her hands, she glanced up at the window above the sink. Her heart nearly stopped beating as she stared at a reflection that wasn't hers.

Chapter 11

"Ellen, what's wrong?" Scott asked his hands on her shoulders.

Ellen couldn't find the words to describe what had just happened to her. She remembered washing dishes and looking into the window only to find the face of a stranger staring back. The girl had appeared pale and filmy, almost translucent, but Ellen was almost certain she was the girl from the locket.

Apparently, she had cried out, though she had no recollection of it. Scott was now staring at her, his eyes clouded with concern.

Finally, she found her voice, "Scott, something is going on in this house. I don't know what, but strange things have been happening. I just saw a girl in the window above the sink."

"What girl? Is she still here?" he asked, already heading for the back door.

"No, she's gone." Ellen said, feeling deflated. Suddenly, her whole body felt weak, no doubt the result of stress and fear. She felt on the verge of crying.

"Well, who in the hell was it?" Scott wanted to know.

Ellen shook her head, "I don't know, honey. I really don't, but I think she's the same girl whose picture I found in a locket hidden in the basement."

Scott stared at her, confusion shadowing his features. Ellen wondered if he was beginning to question his wife's sanity. Could she blame him?

Finally, in a state of emotional turmoil, the events of late taking their toll on her, Ellen slumped into a chair and began to explain everything to her husband. She told him about the basement door opening, the strange mist she had seen, the locket, and her conversation with the Noreen and the research she had conducted on their home. When she had finished, she looked at him expectantly.

Scott slowly shook his head and blew out a long breath, while raking his fingers through his dark hair. Finally, he spoke, "So what are you saying?"

"I don't know. You know I've never really believed in this sort of thing, but I'm beginning to think this house is haunted. Possibly by the girl in the locket, though I haven't a clue who she is." Ellen told her husband, praying he would take her seriously.

"Wow. I don't really know what to say, Ellen. I mean…that's crazy, don't you think?" Scott asked.

Ellen's hopes sank, as she realized her husband didn't believe her. He was probably mentally calculating how quickly the paddy wagon could get to their house. Of course, could she really blame him? The whole thing did sound crazy and this was the first time he was hearing about any of this.

Scott took his wife's silence as an indication that she was considering the possibility that she was wrong. "You're just under a lot of stress, sweetheart. With work, the move, and caring for Natalie, you've just become overwhelmed. Maybe we need to take a little trip somewhere, so that you can relax."

In her heart, Ellen knew that a vacation wouldn't fix whatever was going on in this house. She was also certain that she wasn't crazy. Under stress, yes, but not crazy. Still, she knew that, without more evidence, she would be hard pressed to convince Scott that their house was, indeed, haunted. It was best, at least for now, to let him think she was just stressed. Once she had more evidence, she would try talking to him again.

"You're probably right," she conceded. "Maybe it is stress. I haven't been sleeping well, you know? Maybe I'll call the doctor tomorrow and have him prescribe me something to help me sleep."

"That would probably help." Scott told her, clearly relaxing. "Now, why don't we head

to bed? Things will seem better in the
morning."

She nodded her agreement and allowed
him to help her from her chair. While she stood
in the doorway, he turned off the overhead light
and then gently took her arm and led her
upstairs.

....

Later that night, Ellen lay awake in bed,
staring at the ceiling. Sleep seemed very
unlikely despite the late hour. Glancing at the
clock, Ellen saw that it was well after three in
the morning. Sighing loudly, she turned on her
other side, determined to at least get a few hours
of sleep.

She was just starting to relax when she
heard Natalie screaming loudly from down the
hall. Jumping up, she rushed out of her room
and into her daughter's. Natalie was in her bed,
the blankets tangled and shoved to the foot of
the bed. She was sitting up and Ellen could see
that she was shaking uncontrollably, her hair
matted to her face with sweat.

"Natalie, what's wrong?" Ellen asked,
her voice edged with concern.

Her daughter looked at her then, as if
just realizing she was in the room. Her eyes

were wide and alert, but something in their depths bothered Ellen.

"Baby, did you have a nightmare?" Ellen prodded.

Slowly, Natalie shook her head back and forth. "No, mommy. There was someone in my room. A girl."

Ellen involuntarily sucked in a breath. What the hell did that mean?

"Sweetie, who was in your room? What girl? Is she still here?" Ellen asked, looking around the small room. Though dark, Natalie's night light provided enough illumination to show that the room was empty.

Natalie raised her small, shaky hand and pointed to the end of her bed. "She was standing there, looking at me."

"What did the girl look like?" Ellen asked, already certain of her daughter's answer.

"She was older than me, but younger than you and she had long gold hair like Cinderella." Natalie told her.

Ellen let this information sink in. So, not only was the girl appearing to her, but to her daughter as well. Ellen took little comfort in this. Though this latest development solidified that she was not crazy and seeing things, she did not want her daughter involved in any way.

Natalie began to cry again, and Ellen pulled her daughter into her arms, whispering words of comfort into her ears. "It's okay, Natalie. You'll be fine. That girl can't hurt you." Even as she said the words, however, Ellen wasn't certain if she was telling the truth.

Chapter 12

The next day Ellen called in sick to work. Though they needed the money, she felt her family needed something more important at the moment. She had decided last night, while comforting Natalie back to sleep, that she had to do something to find out who the girl was that had been haunting her house.

After Scott left for work, Ellen dropped Natalie off at daycare. Although she was concerned that the trauma from the night before might have had an effect on her daughter, Natalie had seemed fine at breakfast, even asking for a second slice of French toast. Ellen decided the best thing to do was keep with routine. She had waved goodbye to her daughter and drove off.

Earlier that morning, she had done a quick search for Emily Garritson's boyfriend, Toby Price, but had eventually learned he had moved away to attend college. Apparently, he had never returned because she found no local listing for him in the phone book. Her next step, she decided, was to head to the local police department.

Sitting in the somewhat cramped waiting area of the Crescentville PD, Ellen went over what she was going to say to the detective in charge of the Emily Garritson murder. How could she tell this stranger that she thought a girl haunted her house? She had enough trouble telling her own husband and he hadn't believed her. Would the detective have the same perspective? Would he immediately chalk her story up to mental instability?

"Ms. Christianson?" a male voice called out.

Ellen looked up to see a man in his fifties with thinning gray hair. He was very tall and slightly heavy. His eyes were dark brown and guarded. He was now looking at her expectantly.

"Yes. I'm Mrs. Christianson, but please call me Ellen." She said as she extended her hand. "You must be Detective Crawley."

"I am. The desk sergeant said you had some information pertaining to the Emily Garritson case?" he asked as he shook her hand.

"Um, well, sort of. Is there somewhere we can talk in private?" Ellen asked, aware of several office personnel within earshot.

"Certainly. Follow me to my office." He told her as he led her down a well-lit hallway with several doors on both sides. Although the carpet was well-worn, there appeared to be a fresh coat of paint on the walls. At the end of the hallway, he turned right into a doorway. The nameplate on the door labeled this office as his.

As he took a seat behind a metal desk cluttered with file folders and other office paraphernalia, he indicated with his hand that she should have a seat in the only other available chair.

Once seated, Ellen cleared her throat before she began. "I know this is going to sound a bit bizarre, but I really don't know what else to do. I'm trying to get information about the house my family bought a few months ago."

"Very well, but I'm not sure how I can help you or how this has anything to do with Emily Garritson." Detective Crawley stated, raising a skeptical brow.

"Well, the house I bought is the Garritson house on Owl Creek. I learned through research at the library that the Garritson's daughter, Emily was murdered. Anyway, strange things have been happening in that house. Both my daughter and I have seen a girl. And I found this." Ellen said withdrawing the locket from her purse and handing it to the detective. Though clearly confused, the detective took the locket and looked inside.

"That's the girl my daughter and I have seen. Do you have any idea who she is?" Ellen asked, hoping the detective wouldn't throw her out of his office.

He studied the picture for a moment, withdrew a pair of black framed reading glasses, which he put on, then studied the picture some more. "Where did you get this?"

"In my basement. It was hidden behind one of the stone blocks in our coal room." Ellen explained.

"Hmm. Well, I can't be certain but it looks like a young girl that went missing some time ago. I think her name was Jenny Matthews." He said, still staring at the locket's picture while thoughtfully chewing his bottom lip.

"Did you ever find her?" Ellen asked.

"Um, no. We never did. Her grandparents reported her missing when she didn't return home from the library. She'd been studying with friends, but none of them knew what happened to her. They all left the library around 9:00pm and went their separate ways. According to them, Jenny was headed home. She never got there though. We searched for months, followed up any lead that came our way, but in the end, we never found her." He told her.

"Detective Crawley, I know this is going to sound crazy, but both my daughter and I have seen the girl in that locket. Inside our house." Ellen said with as much certainty as she could muster.

"So, you're telling me Jenny is alive and has been hiding in your house?" He asked, not even bothering to conceal his doubt.

"I'm not so sure she's alive." Ellen said quietly.

"So, what you're telling me is that you believe that Jenny Matthews' ghost is haunting your house? If you don't mind my being frank, ma'am, that sounds a bit ludicrous." The detective stated his voice incredulous.

"I realize that." Ellen said, exasperated. "But it's the truth. There is no other explanation."

"What does this have to do with Emily Garritson?" he wanted to know.

"I'm not sure, but I think the two are tied together. I don't know how or even why I think that, but I do. Were Emily and Jenny friends?" Ellen asked him.

The detective removed his glasses and rubbed the bridge of his nose in the way people do when they have a terrible headache. For a long time, he didn't speak. Finally, he said, "Look, we caught Emily Garritson's murderer and Jenny Matthews went missing a good two or more years before that. So, clearly, the two cases can't be connected. And as far as I know, the two weren't friends. Jenny didn't even live in the area. She was staying here with her grandparents for the summer when she disappeared."

"What if the man you thought killed Emily really didn't do it? What if he was framed?" Ellen asked, knowing that she was beginning to grasp at straws.

Bristling noticeably, the detective asked, "Why on earth would anyone do that? And besides, the man was a convicted sex offender and had Emily's possessions in his trash can." He stated.

"I know. I read about that, but stranger things have happened. And anyway, how did the locket get in my basement?" Ellen demanded.

"Okay. Look, I really think you are making a big deal out of nothing. I'd venture to say that you have been the victim of some local kids playing a prank on you. Hell, Gale Garritson called me several times about similar incidents. I'll come by your place later this evening and have a look around, ok? As for the locket, I'd like to return it to the girl's parents. I have no idea how it got into your basement." He said, already rising from behind his desk, a clear indication that this conversation was finished.

"Very well, detective. Thank you for your time." Ellen said as she rose from her chair. She knew a send-off when she got one.

"Ms. Christianson," he began, "I really do believe this is a prank. Kids are always pulling these stunts, especially in semi-rural areas like yours. They can sneak around without anyone taking notice. I promise I'll look your place over and see if I can find any footprints or other evidence that will prove my theory. In the meantime, call me if you have any other disturbances."

He had already moved to the door and was gesturing with his arm that she should leave. Ellen said goodbye and moved down the hall and out the front door. Frustration couldn't begin to describe how she felt.

....

Later that afternoon, Ellen sat in her kitchen, sipping a glass of tea, mulling over her conversation with Detective Crawley. How could he be so certain the incidents that took place in her house were the result of teenage pranks? Not to mention, how could he dismiss the locket of a missing girl turning up in a house the girl had supposedly never stepped foot in?

Just then, her phone rang. Aggravated by the interruption, Ellen took her time going to the phone. "Hello."

"Ellen, it's me. Marcie. How are you?" Ellen's friend asked cheerfully.

"Oh, Marcie, it's good to hear from you. I'm doing fine. How are you?" Ellen asked, truthfully happy to hear from her friend.

"Well, I just flew in from London and thought I'd come over and visit. I haven't seen the new house yet and we have so much to catch up on. Maybe we could have dinner." Marcie said more as a statement than a question.

Ellen laughed at her friend's excitement. "Sure, Marcie. What time can you be here?"

Marcie explained that she had a few things to take care of at the airlines but could be at Ellen's house by 5:00pm. Ellen agreed and gave her directions. They hung up, both anticipating the reunion.

....

"Wow, Ellen. This house is great!" Marcie exclaimed as she looked around the living room.

"Thanks." Ellen said, regarding her friend. As usual, Marcie looked fantastic. She was wearing faded designer jeans that hugged her curves, a short-sleeved cream scoop neck top, and brown leather boots. Her blonde hair was pulled back in a stylish bun, revealing her high cheekbones and flawless complexion.

Marcie picked up a recent photo of Natalie off the fireplace mantel and remarked,

"She's getting so big. I can't believe how much she looks like you."

Ellen smiled. She was more than a little thankful that Natalie favored her mother and not her dead-beat father. Not that Joey Jacobs had been a bad-looking guy, but Ellen thought it was easier for Scott to accept Natalie since she looked like his wife, not some man he had never met.

Ellen watched as Marcie continued to wander around the living room, occasionally pausing to regard a photo or study the view from the windows. "What's down the hall?" Ellen heard her friend ask.

"Oh, that's the kitchen, which is my favorite part of the house. It's so bright and cheerful." Ellen answered, following her friend towards the kitchen.

Marcie stopped short of the kitchen, gasping slightly.

"Marcie, what's wrong?" Ellen asked, fear seizing her body. What could it be this time?

Chapter 13

"Oh, God, Ellen. I think I just saw a mouse run across the floor." Marcie said.

Ellen's body relaxed immediately. Though she hated rodents, this latest problem seemed mundane and somewhat of a relief in comparison to the other issues that plagued her. She found herself suddenly laughing.

Marcie stared at her in disbelief. "Do you find this funny?" her friend asked, trying to sound put off. A smile, however, tugged at the corners of her mouth. "I thought you hated mice."

"I do, but if you could've seen the look on your face." Ellen said, her words interrupted by her uncontrolled giggles.

"Well, if I were you, I'd call in an exterminator promptly." Marcie said, trying to maintain her composure. "I've heard mice multiple like...well...like mice."

At that moment, both women broke into hysterical laughter. Ellen, unable to hold herself up, slumped to the floor. Marcie remained standing, but was bent over holding her belly.

"My sides hurt." Marcie managed to say. This sent both women into another uncontrolled fit of laughter. After several moments, however, the giggling began to die down and Ellen was finally able to stand again.

"Ok. That was funny. I really needed that. I've been under so much stress lately." Ellen told her friend. "And as for an exterminator, here he comes now."

Both women watched in amusement as Boo sauntered into the kitchen from behind them. He stopped and sniffed the air, then crept across the floor quietly, positioning himself in front of the stove. His gaze could've burned holes in the linoleum it was so intense.

"Yeah, I think he's got it under control." Marcie agreed. "Come on, let's go to dinner."

....

"This steak is to die for!" Marcie said, her mouth full.

"It can't be as good as this salmon. It practically melts in your mouth." Ellen told her friend between bites.

They had decided on *Vincent's*, an upscale eatery located a few miles from Ellen's house. Both had ordered white wine with their meals and Ellen was feeling a little giddy from its effects.

"Oh, Marcie. I'm so glad you're here. This has been so much fun." Ellen said as she polished off the last of her salmon and rice.

"I know what you mean. We hardly ever get a chance to hang out. I know it's mostly my fault cause of my job. Actually, I wanted to talk to you about that. I've been thinking of leaving the airline. My cousin Jesse has asked me to start a party planning business with her. I know it's risky, but I wouldn't have to travel so much. Maybe I could finally settle down, find a decent man, you know?" Marcie said.

Ellen digested what her friend had just told her. "Marcie, I don't know what to say. I mean, of course I want you here, but I thought you loved travelling."

"I do, Ell, but I'm getting older. I see what you have-Scott, Natalie and the house-and I want those same things too. You know, a place to call home and a loving, supportive family." Marcie told her, emotion breaking in her voice.

Ellen was a little taken aback. She had never pictured Marcie as the settling down type. She was relieved to hear it though. Having a close friend nearby would be wonderful. She told Marcie just as much.

"So you think I should do it?' Marcie asked.

"Well, yeah. I mean, if that's what you want, I think you should do it. Does Jesse have any experience in the party planning field?" Ellen wanted to know.

"Not exactly, but she has a degree in business and she's really smart. She seems to think we can do it."

"Then go for it." Ellen said, raising her glass for a toast. "To a successful future!"

....

The women returned home just after 10pm. Marcie had agreed to stay the night with Ellen rather than at her hotel. The house was dark which suggested Scott and Natalie were already asleep. Ellen pressed her finger to her lips, indicating they should be quiet. Marcie nodded and they entered the house.

Heading directly to the kitchen, Ellen went to the refrigerator and pulled out two bottles of beer. Despite the late hour, she wasn't tired and wanted to sit up and talk for a while longer.

"I wonder if your cat had any success ridding your home of unsavory visitors?" Marcie asked as she accepted the beer Ellen offered.

Glancing around the kitchen, Ellen didn't see any evidence of a battle. "I don't know. I'd hate to think of anything being killed, but I have to admit I don't want the little creatures taking up residence in the cupboards either."

Suddenly, the kitchen light flickered off. Left in total darkness, both women sat motionless, unsure of what to do.

"Did the power go out?" Marcie asked.

"I guess so." Ellen said. "I'm going to try the switch."

Moving in the direction of the switch, Ellen felt along the wall until she reached the switch. *Weird.* She thought. The switch was in the down position. Flipping it up, the overhead light came back on.

"Oh, thank God. I couldn't imagine spending the night without electricity." Marcie said.

"I know what you mean." Ellen replied, making her way back to the table.

No sooner had she sat down, the light went out again. The kitchen plunged into darkness once more.

"Dammit!" Ellen cursed, getting up again to find the light switch.

"What's going on, Ell? Why's the power going on and off?" Marcie asked.

"It's not. The switch was turned off. And it is again." She told her friend as she flipped the switch to the on position. Again, light flooded the kitchen.

Marcie seemed to consider this but didn't comment further. Rather, she sat quietly at the table, sipping her beer.

After a few moments of silence, Ellen broached a subject she was apprehensive to discuss. Despite her many years of friendship with Marcie, she wasn't sure how the other woman would react. Sure, they'd goofed off as kids, telling ghost stories and things of that nature, but they'd never really had a serious discussion on the matter. "I think my house is haunted."

At first, it seemed Marcie hadn't heard her because she remained silent. Ellen stared at her expecting her to burst out laughing or tell her she belonged in the loony bin. Finally, she said very matter-of-factly. "I know."

"What?" Ellen said, almost too stunned to speak. That was not the response she had been expecting.

Marcie took a drink of her beer and scooted her chair closer to the table. She tilted her head thoughtfully to the side and began peeling at the edge of the label on her beer. The silence was almost unbearable as Ellen waited for her friend to explain what she meant.

"Ellen, we've been friends for a long time, right?" Marcie asked.

"Uh, yeah. Since high school. You were the only one I ever felt connected with." Ellen told her.

"Ok. Well, there's something I've never confided in you. I always wanted to, but you seemed so grounded. I thought you would laugh at me or think I was some kind of whacko. So…I just never mentioned it." Marcie said, pausing to take another big gulp of beer.

"I knew the moment I walked in the door that something wasn't right here. I could feel it in the air, almost like the air was too thick…or too heavy maybe. Also, there was something that made my skin tingle like when someone's watching you. Do you know that feeling?"

Ellen stared at her friend completely dumbfounded. Of course she knew that feeling. She'd been familiar with it since the moment she stepped foot in this house. She managed to nod at her friend to let her know she understood.

"Well, I've recognized that sensation before…in other houses. Throughout my whole life, I've had feelings, seen things, and heard things. Things that couldn't be explained, you know? Anyway, I've learned to pick up on the signs. Sometimes I even…know things. It's like someone just implants the information into my brain and I just know." Marcie said. She stopped talking and looked at Ellen for some kind of confirmation that she understood.

"Wow. I never knew. You could've told me, Marcie. I never would've laughed at you. What's funny though is that since this has been happening to me, I feel the same way.

Like people are going to think I'm nuttier than a fruitcake. What kinds of things do you sense?" Ellen asked.

"It depends. Some energies are stronger than others. That's all a haunting really is, you know. It's leftover energy. It tells a story. Sometimes the energy is faint and you can only pick up on some things. Other times, the energy is strong and you can almost read it like a book. It tells the story of what happened." Marcie said matter-of-factly as she finished off her beer.

"Can you tell what happened here?" Ellen wanted to know, getting up to fetch another beer from the fridge for her friend.

Taking the beer, Marcie continued, "Bits and pieces. But not the whole picture. I can tell you this though. There is nothing to fear from the girl. She is not trying to harm you. She just wants peace. She doesn't understand what's happened to her. Well, I shouldn't say that. She knows she's dead and she knows how it happened, but she doesn't understand why she's…stuck here."

"Well that's a relief, I guess. All this time I've been frightened half to death." Ellen stated.

"But Ellen, she could become desperate." Marcie said, reaching for Ellen's hand, "After that, I don't know what may happen."

Now Ellen was scared. She could feel the hairs rise up on the back of her neck. "You mean she may try to hurt us?"

Marcie nodded, still holding her friend's hand, offering whatever comfort she could. "I don't know for sure. I don't think she'd hurt you intentionally, but she may become more frantic in her attempts to get your attention. I think her name is Jenny." Marcie said.

Ellen was in awe of her friend. She believed her completely because there was no way Marcie could've known the name of the girl in the locket. There was no way she could have known any of it.

"So, what do I do?" Ellen asked.

"I don't know, Ell. But you have to do something. The energy in this house is strong and I fear things are going to get worse before they get better." Marcie said, her voice wavering slightly.

"But why is she here? I haven't been able to find any kind of a connection between her disappearance and this house." Ellen wanted to know.

"I don't know. Most of it's too fuzzy to get a clear picture." Marcie answered.

For a long time, neither woman spoke. Finally, Ellen told her friend that they needed to talk to someone about this. Marcie agreed. After a few more minutes' discussion, Ellen convinced Marcie to sleep on the floor with her in Natalie's room. Though difficult, both women managed to fall into a fitful sleep.

Chapter 14

The next morning, Ellen told Marcie she had to go to work but planned to leave early that afternoon. In the meantime, Marcie was going to head to the local bookstore and pick up some books on hauntings and ghosts. They would meet for lunch at 1pm.

Ellen dropped Natalie off at daycare with a promise to take her to the park that evening. The park was hosting "Pioneer Days" and Natalie wanted to see all the different costumes from that era.

Once at the office, the day passed at a snail's pace. Ellen couldn't seem to keep her mind on her work. More than once, her boss had to remind her to type up an important letter he needed for a court appearance that afternoon. Finally, around noon, Ellen announced that she needed to leave early. Her boss, always very understanding, didn't ask any questions and told her to go.

In her car, Ellen found it difficult to keep focused on her driving. Her mind kept spinning in every direction. She couldn't wait to see what Marcie found out. For the first time since this all began, Ellen had an ally. She no longer had to go it alone and that made her feel like she could face this problem head on.

Arriving at the appointed restaurant, Ellen spotted Marcie's car in the parking lot. Heading inside, Ellen told the hostess she was there to meet her friend. The hostess smiled politely and showed Ellen to the table where Marcie eagerly waited.

Once the hostess was out of earshot, Marcie began talking in a hushed tone. "I took it upon myself to make us an appointment with a local medium."

"What?" Ellen asked.

Before Marcie could answer, the waitress arrived for the drink order. Ellen asked for water with lemon, while Marcie got a diet coke. They also went ahead and put in their lunch order for a grilled chicken salad with Balsamic Vinaigrette dressing. They watched as the waitress sauntered away.

"What exactly does a medium do?" Ellen asked, a little embarrassed about her lack of knowledge.

"Basically they communicate with the dead." Marcie told her.

"Hmmm." Ellen said thoughtfully. "But isn't that what you do?"

Marcie shook her head. "No. I have no control over whatever it is that I do. I kinda just pick up on things here and there. But nothing concrete. Accomplished mediums know *how* to use their gift. Sometimes, they alone can convince a spirit to leave a person's home. I thought it was worth a shot to at least talk to someone."

"Ok. You're right. It's worth a try." Ellen told her friend.

"Good. I'm glad that's settled." Marcie said, smiling happily.

"So, what did you find out at the bookstore?" Ellen wanted to know.

Marcie reached down beside her chair and pulled up a bag. Carefully, she selected one of the books and pulled it out. "This book is about another woman whose family faced a similar situation to yours. I didn't get a chance to read the whole thing, of course, but what I did read sounded promising."

Ellen took the book and began skimming through the pages.

"This book is a compiled list of exorcisms performed on houses. I don't know how accurate it is, but we have to start somewhere." Marcie said as she handed Ellen the second book. "The rest of the books I have are just about hauntings in general."

Just then, the food arrived. Though Ellen wasn't very hungry, she knew she needed to eat. Besides, the salads looked delicious. Already, Marcie had drizzled dressing all over hers and was taking a huge bite.

"What time is the appointment with the medium?" Ellen asked.

"Two this afternoon. She's going to meet us at your house." Marcie answered.

"What's her name?" Ellen wanted to know.

"Her name is Alex Bellows." Marcie told her.

For the remainder of the meal, the women ate in silence, each of their minds going over their upcoming meeting with the medium. After their plates were cleared away and the bill was paid, they both headed out the door. They drove separately back to Ellen's house. They would have just enough time to meet with the medium before Scott got home and Ellen had to pick up Natalie from daycare.

....

No sooner had the women pulled their cars into the circular driveway in front of Ellen's house, another car drove up. The car was a newer white Dodge Caravan. The driver put the car into park, and then slowly got out.

"I hope I'm in the right place." The woman called out cheerily. "I'm looking for Ellen Christianson."

"I'm Ellen. Are you Ms. Bellows?"

"Yes. But you can call me Alex."
The woman told her.

The woman began to approach the porch. Ellen guessed her to be in her late fifties to early sixties. Her hair, probably once blonde, was now a light shade of gray with touches of white at the temples. She had twinkling blue eyes and rosy cheeks. A touch on the plump side, she wore a pale blue button down shirt, khakis, and white tennis shoes. The woman looked the perfect part for a grandmother, not someone who could speak to the dead.

As she reached Ellen and Marcie, she extended her hand. "Pleased to meet you."

Ellen returned the handshake and introduced Marcie.

"Oh, yes. You're the woman I spoke to on the phone. But this is your house, correct?" she asked, turning her attention back to Ellen.

"Yes. I don't know how much Marcie told you, but my husband and I bought the house back in March. Since then, we've been experiencing…strange things. Well, mainly *I've* had the experiences, though my daughter has also seen the…uh…ghost." Ellen explained, feeling a little embarrassed admitting her house was haunted to a complete stranger.

"I see. Well, do you mind if I come in and take a look?" Alex inquired. "You can finish explaining what's happened once I get a feel for the house."

Ellen nodded and together she and Marcie led the older woman into the house.

"Where have most of the events taken place?" Alex asked.

"There have been incidents throughout the house," Ellen explained, "but mostly in the kitchen and basement area."

Ellen led Alex down the hall to the kitchen, which looked remarkably bright and cheery and *unremarkably* haunted.

"Is this the basement door?" the older woman asked, indicating the door that led downstairs.

"Yes, it is. I rarely go down there anymore because it scares me. My husband does the laundry and scoops the litterbox, which is also in the basement." Ellen explained.

"Hmmm...yes." The woman said with no further explanation, her right hand pressed against the door and her eyes closed.

Ellen and Marcie glanced at one another, unsure of what was happening. Would the woman go into some kind of trance and begin chanting some ritualistic babble? They both waited expectantly for something to happen.

Alex opened her eyes and smiled reassuringly at the other two women. "Ok then. I'm going to walk around the rest of the house,

if you don't mind. When I'm finished, I'd
like to go down there." She told them tilting her
head in the direction of the basement.

"Do you want us to come with you?"
Marcie asked.

"No, dear. I'd prefer to walk through the
house alone and see what I can pick up on.
Afterwards, we'll talk." She told them and
started down the hall towards the living room.

Ellen and Marcie were left alone in the
kitchen. With nothing else to do, they sat down
at the kitchen table to wait. The silence
stretched out before them, the only sound was
the ticking of the wall clock above the table.

"What do you think she's doing?"
Marcie finally asked.

"I don't have a clue. I guess she's
just…feeling the place out." Ellen answered.

"You think we should go spy on her?"
Marcie asked, only half joking.

Ellen smiled at her friend. Even though
the situation was a serious one, Marcie was
trying her best to ease the stress. Once again,
Ellen found herself thanking her lucky stars for
such a good friend.

"I think she's upstairs now." Marcie
commented while flipping through a *Glamour*
magazine.

"Yeah, I heard the stairs creaking a few
minutes ago." Ellen responded.

"Dear God, would you ever wear those?" Marcie asked, pushing the magazine over to reveal a rail thin girl wearing five-inch platform boots.

"Uh…no." Ellen said, distracted.

Sometime later, Alex returned to the kitchen. "Ok, ladies. I'm ready to go into the basement now."

Ellen stood up. "Do you need us to do anything?"

"No, sweetie. I'll just be a few minutes." Alex told her, as she opened the basement door and headed down the stairs.

The seconds stretched into minutes. Neither Marcie nor Ellen could hear anything from the basement. More than once, Marcie snuck over to the open basement door and peered down the stairs.

"I can't see her." She whispered to Ellen from across the kitchen.

"Marcie, get over here and sit down!" Ellen reprimanded her friend lightly.

"I just want to know what's going on." Marcie replied as she reluctantly crept back to the kitchen table where Ellen sat waiting.

No sooner had she taken her seat when Alex returned to the kitchen. At first, the older woman said nothing. She seemed to be collecting her thoughts, her left hand propped atop the counter.

"Alex, is everything ok?" Ellen asked, rising from her chair.

The woman looked at her and smiled. "Yes, dear. Please sit down so we can discuss this."

It could be Ellen's imagination, but the woman looked somehow drained. Though she smiled, it seemed dimmer than before. Had something happened to change the woman's cheerful demeanor?

"I've been so rude, Alex. Can I offer you something to drink?" Ellen asked as she got up to check the contents of the fridge. "We have water, iced tea, juice. Any of those sound good?"

"Actually, dear, I could go for a spot of brandy if you have it." Alex said.

Taken aback, Ellen replied, "Um, I think my husband keeps a bottle of bourbon around here somewhere. Will that be ok?"

"That'll be lovely. Thank you." Alex told her.

Ellen busied herself looking through the cabinets for her husband's "secret" stash of liquor. In the back of the cabinet above the fridge, Ellen discovered a bottle three quarters full of bourbon. Taking out three glasses, she poured a healthy shot's worth in each and carried the glasses over to the table.

"Here you go." Ellen said, handing one glass to Alex and one to Marcie.

"Oh, thank you. This is heavenly." Alex said and then downed the entire glass.

"Would you like more?" Ellen asked, incredulous.

"Maybe a spot more." The woman answered.

Ellen fetched the bottle and filled the woman's glass again, leaving the bottle sit on the table just in case. Either the woman had experienced something truly unsettling or she was a closet boozer. Either way, Ellen decided to leave the liquor within arm's length.

"So Alex, what happened? Did you sense anything?" Marcie asked.

The woman blew out a long breath and ran her fingers through her shortly cropped hair. "Oh, yes. I sensed something alright. You know, in all my years of doing this, I've never felt such deep despair. And anger…"

Ellen grabbed the woman's hand. "What do you mean, Alex?"

"There is a heavy feeling of sadness, anger, even mild hostility in this house." She said matter-of-factly.

"Can it hurt us?" Marcie asked, worry fringing her words.

Alex shook her head and shrugged. "I don't know for sure, but I don't think that is the intention."

"But who *is* it?" Ellen demanded.

Again, Alex shrugged. "It's a young woman…or girl actually with golden hair. I've dealt with difficult spirits that don't want to listen to me, but in the end, I've always gotten through to them. But this one, it's as if she doesn't want to listen. I don't know why."

"What does it mean? Is it Jenny Matthews?" Ellen asked, more to herself than to the two women at the table.

"Yes, Jenny is her name. Oh, that poor girl. So much pain and regret. She's lost. Completely lost." Alex informed them, tears brimming in her eyes.

"But how did she die? And who killed her?" Marcie pushed.

Alex pulled a hankie from her pocket and blotted her eyes. "I could see her death plainly. She was strangled to death. It was horrible. She was so scared and didn't understand why it was happening to her. I think it happened here. In this house. That's why she's so reluctant to leave. And over the years, she's become…resentful almost. It's going to take some time to get through to her. She doesn't trust us yet."

"According to Detective Crawley, she was never in this house and didn't know the previous owners. What happened to her body?" Ellen wanted to know. "The police said they never found her body after she went missing."

"I just don't know, dear. I couldn't see the killer. It's as if Jenny has blocked his identity out." Alex said, sounding deflated.

"It's okay, Alex. You did your best." Marcie said soothingly.

"So how are we going to find out the truth? I want to help Jenny. I really do. But I can't keep living like this. Something has to give, or Scott and I are going to have to sell the house." Ellen said, clearly frustrated.

For several moments, no one spoke. Then, Alex offered, "There is one thing I can think of. It's not without risk, though."

"What?" Ellen and Marcie said in unison.

"Have the house blessed. It may help ward off some of the negativity and help Jenny feel safer." Alex said.

"Blessed? You mean by a priest?" Ellen asked.

"A priest could do it, but you can do it yourself as well."

"How would we go about that? Don't you have to be religious or something?" Marcie asked.

Alex shook her head. "It's easy. Just get some sage and burn it in each room, while repeating a kind of prayer over and over. It doesn't have to be a religious prayer. Just something like 'bless this house and keep it safe from harm'. It's possible Jenny still feels threatened by her killer and that's why she won't communicate. Fear is a huge obstacle to overcome. A blessing could make her feel safer"

"What if it doesn't work?" Inquired Marcie.

"It may not, but it's worth a try. If you don't think you can do it, contact a local church." Alex informed them.

"But neither my husband nor I have attended church in years, though we were both raised Catholic. How will that work?" Ellen wanted to know.

"Have faith, dear. That's how it will work." Alex told her, smiling reassuringly and squeezing her hand.

Abruptly, the older woman stood.

"Do you need to be going?" Ellen asked.

"I'm afraid so. My granddaughter will be arriving soon and I need to be home to greet her." Alex answered.

Ellen and Marcie walked Alex to the door, saying their goodbyes and thanking her.

"Please call me, dear, and let me know what happens." Alex said jotting down her cell phone number on a piece of paper.

"I will. I promise. And again, thank you for everything." Ellen said, giving the woman a hug.

Once she was gone, Ellen turned to Marcie, "I have to go pick up Natalie. She wants to go to the park afterwards. Besides, Scott will be home soon. We mustn't say a word to him about this. Not yet anyway. He just won't understand."

"Ok. What do you want me to do?" Marcie asked.

"If you don't mind, go to the library. Find out as much as you can about blessing houses and what we need to do. It's important we know what we're up against. Tomorrow is Friday. We can do the blessing then. Scott won't get home until after 6:00. He always works late on Fridays. I can get out of work by 4:00. Will that work?" Ellen asked.

"That sounds good. I'm going to stay at my mom's tonight. She's called me like a thousand times wanting me to come over. We can meet here tomorrow at 4:15?"

"Ok. Thanks Marcie." Ellen told her friend.

Chapter 15

Ellen was extremely busy at work the next day. Her boss was starting a criminal trial on Monday and needed a lot of last-minute documents to be filed. Though it was difficult to keep her mind on task, she managed to complete everything and was ready to leave by 4:00 as she had planned.

On the way home, she stopped at a local store that specialized in spiritual goods and herbal remedies. Ellen purchased the sage that Alex had recommended and then made her way home. Marcie was already waiting in the driveway.

"You ready to do this?" Marcie asked as Ellen climbed out of her car.

"I think so. I got the sage. I hope it's the right kind. They had a surprisingly large selection." She told her friend.

Together, they went inside. Neither woman was really sure what to say, but they decided on an appropriate prayer and began the blessing upstairs. They figured they would start there and then make there way downstairs and then finally bless the basement last.

As each room was blessed, Ellen began to feel more confident. She began to really believe in the words she was saying. She truly wanted her home to be safe for her family and she wanted Jenny to be able to move on and be at peace.

They finished upstairs and made their way down the stairs, careful to bless them as well. Once downstairs, they blessed the living room, dining room, and kitchen. Ellen paused at the top of the basement steps. She felt unsettled going down there, but knew she had to.

"Go on Ell. You've got this." Marcie nudged her friend and offered her a reassuring smile.

They made their way down the steps and into the main part of the basement. Together, the two women began repeating the same prayer they had used throughout the rest of the house.

"Bless this house and keep us safe from harm." They said in unison.

Ellen fanned the sage outwards into the room.

They continued around the basement, blessing each corner, the furnace room, and finally the old coal room. As Ellen finished fanning the sage in the last corner of the coal room, something in the air changed. The air around them became thick and heavy, almost tangible. Also, the temperature began to drop considerably. Ellen hadn't noticed it before, but now she could see her breath fogging up.

"What's going on?" Marcie asked.

"I don't know. It's getting really cold in here. Come on. Let's get out of her." Ellen said as she started towards the open door.

Suddenly and without warning, the door swung shut. The two women were incased in near darkness except for the burning ember on the sage.

"Marcie, what happened?" Ellen asked, her words tinged with fear.

"I'm not sure. The door just slammed shut on its own." Marcie said, reaching her hand out to grasp Ellen's.

Pulling Ellen along behind her, Marcie made her way to the door, turning the knob as she reached it. "It won't turn!"

"What?" Ellen said, a new jolt of fear coursing through her.

Pushing Marcie out of the way, Ellen tried the doorknob. No matter how hard she tried, though, it wouldn't turn. Not a single inch. It was as if it was glued shut. She began pushing on the door with all her might, mentally willing it to open. Still, it remained closed tight.

As the two women struggled with the door, the temperature in the room continued to grow colder. Ellen's fingers were starting to grow numb in the chilling temperature. She struggled to grip the doorknob, her breath coming out in ragged gasps. Tears began to

stream down her face from fear and
frustration. She was moments away from panic
taking over.

The sage burned out at this point, Ellen
having dropped it on the ground in her attempts
to open the door. The two women were plunged
into complete darkness. The temperature was so
cold by this point, Ellen's body began to
tremble.

Sagging to the floor, Ellen slumped
against the door, tears pouring down her cheeks.
She was sobbing uncontrollably. Marcie sank
down beside her and wrapped her arms around
Ellen as much to help warm her as to offer her
comfort.

The sound of a soft, almost distant voice
filled the room. With each passing moment, it
grew in intensity and volume. Though the voice
was soft and whispery, the words were clear.
Help me. Please. Help me.

"Oh, my God!" Marcie said.

A fresh wave of terror seized Ellen. She
fought for control over her emotions, but she
was so frightened, all she could do was sit there,
her back against the door. She wrapped her
arms around her knees and placed her hands
over her ears. Finally, when she could take it no
more, she screamed. "Stop it! Leave us alone!"

No sooner had the words parted her lips,
the door flew open, propelling Ellen and Marcie

backwards and into the main part of the basement. For a moment, both women lay in a tangled heap on the floor. Marcie was the first to react, "Ellen, get up!" she exclaimed, pulling on her friend's arm, willing her to stand up.

Reality sank in, and Ellen leapt to her feet. Together the two women fled from the basement. They didn't stop running until they were both safely outside.

"What the hell just happened in there?" Marcie demanded, as she struggled to catch her breath.

Still too rattled to speak, Ellen just shook her head.

"There was someone in there with us, Ellen." Marcie stated.

Her eyes brimming with fresh tears, Ellen collapsed on the porch steps. "I know Marcie. I heard it. And felt it. What am I going to do?"

"It's time to call in a professional. We need someone with more faith and knowledge to bless this house." Marcie told her.

Ellen nodded. "I know. I'll contact my old church, the one I attended when I was younger."

"Ok. We have to get someone out here. And soon. Alex said things might intensify and boy was she right." Marcie said.

"I'm not going back in that house until Scott gets home." Ellen stated.

"I agree. I'll wait here with you until he gets here."

....

Later that evening, Ellen phoned St. John's church and made an appointment for the following day to meet with the priest.

She didn't tell Scott what had happened. It was pointless really. He would have chalked it up to their overactive imaginations and threw in a drafty basement for good measure. But Ellen knew that neither she nor Marcie had imagined what had happened. And she also knew that a draft hadn't caused the door to slam shut and refuse to open.

Throughout the evening, she tried to appear normal. She made baked chicken and dressing for dinner and then played Memory with Natalie at the dining room table. At bedtime, she tucked Natalie into bed and told Scott she didn't feel well and was turning in early.

"Hope you're not coming down with something." He told her as she started up the stairs. "I'll be up shortly. I just have some paperwork I need to finish up."

Alone in the dark, Ellen contemplated her next move. She would meet with the priest and do her best to explain the strange and frightening occurrences in her home. She would plead with him to come bless the house immediately. She was also going to have to do more research and find out just exactly what happened to Jenny Matthews the night she died.

Chapter 16

"Hi, we're here to see Father Donovan."
Ellen told the strikingly attractive woman that
greeted them when she and Marcie entered the
church. Dark hair hung loosely around her
shoulders and trailed down her back. A perfect
oval face, fair skin and dark almond shaped eyes
created a look of mystery, while a figure most
supermodels would envy completed the picture.

"I'm Danielle." The woman told them as
she led them down a darkened hallway towards
the back of the church. "I'm Father Donovan's
personal assistant. I've been with the church for
almost fifteen years."

"Hubba, hubba." Marcie whispered
under her breath. "I wonder why Father
Donovan keeps her around."

Ellen shot her friend a look.

It had been years since Ellen had
attended church at St. John's. The place hadn't
changed much. Danielle must have started
working for the church shortly after Ellen quit
attending.

"Father Donovan will be delighted to see
you again after so long." Danielle told them,
flashing another bright smile as she stopped in
front of an open door at the end of the hall.

Ellen and Marcie stepped forward into
the small but cozy office. Behind a sturdy,

well-used wooden desk, Father Donovan stood to greet them. In his 50's, Father Donovan was tall and athletic with salt and pepper hair combed back from his face and bright blue eyes that crinkled when he smiled. Overall, a good-looking man. His smile was quick and inviting. He beckoned for them to take a seat in the two chairs on the opposite side of his desk.

"Ellen, it's so good to see you again. Danielle tells me you want to come back to the church. Naturally, we're delighted." Father Donovan said, clasping his hands in front of him.

Ellen wasn't sure how to begin. She had arranged the meeting earlier that morning and remained vague when asked what it was about. She had eluded that she was interested in rejoining the church after a long hiatus, but had some concerns she would like addressed first.

"Father Donovan, this is difficult for me to say. I wasn't completely honest about the nature of this meeting. You see, my husband and I bought a house a few months ago, and since we moved in we've been having…issues."

"What sort of issues?" the priest asked, his interest clearly piqued.

Ellen decided to dive right in, "I think my home is haunted, Father. I don't know how else to describe it. Since my family moved in, strange things have been happening and I fear for our safety. I think there's some kind of…spirit in my home, a girl that died some time ago. I think she's lost and can't find her way. She was murdered, though I have no proof other than the word of a medium we had over."

Father Donovan stared at her, a mixture of confusion and disbelief clouding his handsome features. "I see. What is it exactly that you want me to do?"

Again, Ellen and Marcie looked at one another, unsure of how to explain.

Marcie cleared her throat and said, "We were hoping you could bless the house. As soon as possible."

"I see." Said Father Donovan. "Well, I must say, I didn't see this one coming."

"We know this seems crazy, but we really don't know what else to do."

The priest appeared to be contemplating what he'd been told. Most likely, he had never had to deal with this sort of thing and was unsure how to proceed. Marcie and Ellen waited patiently for him to comment.

Finally, he seemed to make up his mind, "House blessing are common. That won't be an issue. I'm pretty booked up, however. I could make it perhaps in two weeks?"

"I was hoping it could be sooner?"
Ellen asked. She didn't want to be pushy, but
something had to be done.

"Very well. On your way out, see
Danielle. She can make an appointment for
some time Monday." The priest answered,
perhaps sensing her distress.

The two women stood up. Monday it
would have to be.

"Thank you, Father." Ellen told him.

As instructed, on the way out they
stopped by Danielle's desk and made the
necessary arrangements for Father Donovan to
come bless Ellen's home Monday at 11:00am.

....

Later that night, Ellen awoke with a
start. Lying in the darkness, she listened
carefully for the source of her abrupt departure
from sleep. The only sounds she could make
out were Scott's even breathing and the flutter
of the ceiling fan whirling above the bed.

After several moments, she decided to
go check on Natalie. Earlier in the evening, the
little girl had complained of an upset stomach.
Ellen was concerned that maybe her daughter
was sick and had called out to her. Getting out
of bed, Ellen trudged down the hall to her
daughter's open bedroom door. To her surprise,

however, Natalie's bed was unoccupied, the covers cast aside in a tangled heap.

"Natalie?" Ellen called out in a hushed tone, so as not to awaken Scott.

There was no answer, so Ellen checked the bathroom, which was also empty. Where could the little girl have gone to? Perhaps she had slipped downstairs to get a drink of juice. Ellen made her way downstairs, bumping her knee on the banister as she went. Cursing to herself, she rubbed her knee to dull the throbbing and continued on to the kitchen.

The kitchen light was off, but the refrigerator door hung open, casting a dim yellow triangle of light across the center of the kitchen floor. Ellen's eyes darted to the basement door. It was in its usual cracked position, but the back door was hanging open. Ellen's heart seemed to stop momentarily as she realized Natalie must have gone outside.

Ellen raced to the door and ran outside. The moon was high above, affording Ellen some illumination to see by. She frantically looked around for her missing daughter. At first, she saw nothing, but then the outline of a small figure began to take shape near the edge of the lake.

"Natalie!" Ellen screamed, her voice still hoarse from sleep.

The child either didn't hear her or chose to ignore her because she continued to stand on the sloping edge of the lake. She appeared to be staring into the inky black water.

Her legs trembling with fear, Ellen managed to pick up her pace and she ran to the water's edge. Gratefully, she grabbed hold of Natalie's arm, yanking her back away from the lake's treacherous waters.

"Natalie, what are you doing?" Ellen demanded.

The little girl shook her head slightly and her eyes focused up on her mother's face. "Mommy, what's wrong?"

"Honey, why did you come out here?" Ellen asked, her tone softening at the confused expression on her daughter's face.

"I wanted a drink of juice, cause my throat hurt, so I went to the kitchen. Then I saw the girl. She wanted me to come with her to the lake." Natalie answered, tears welling in her eyes. "Did I do something wrong, mommy?"

"Oh, baby." Ellen said, pulling the little girl into her arms. "Was it the girl from your room?"

"Yes, mommy. Her name is Jenny. She's very nice. Sometimes she plays with me in my room." Natalie answered, still sniffling.

At this, Ellen's body went rigid. "When does she play with you?"

"When I'm alone in my room, after you and Scott go to bed." The little girl answered.

"Come on, baby. Let's get back inside." Ellen said, taking her daughter's hand in hers and leading her back towards the house. She couldn't help glancing over her shoulder towards the lake. For a fleeting moment, it looked like a hazy figure stood on the opposite side of the lake. When Ellen blinked, however, the image disappeared.

Back inside, Ellen tucked Natalie back in bed, and then crawled in beside her. There was no way she was leaving Natalie alone tonight. Jenny might be a benevolent spirit, but Ellen found it entirely too creepy for her daughter to be playing with a ghost. She had to find out what happened to Jenny before it was too late.

....

The next day was Sunday. At the kitchen table, in the early morning hours, Ellen told Scott about Natalie's late night journey to the lake. She also told him Natalie's explanation for why she'd gone out there.

"Ellen, honey, Natalie is a child. It's not uncommon for kids to have make-believe friends. When I was a kid, I remember I had an imaginary friend named Ed. I used to do everything with him, but I finally realized he wasn't real. I'm sure that's what Natalie is going through." Scott said.

This just further frustrated Ellen. Why was her husband so reluctant to believe their house was haunted? "Scott, are you going to sit here and tell me that nothing strange has happened to you since we moved into this house?"

Scott rolled his eyes. "Are we back on this? Sweetheart, there are no such things as ghosts. The strange things that seem to happen to you are no doubt a direct result of your overactive imagination. I mean, it's normal to feel creeped out in a new house, right? But to conclude it's haunted is a bit far reaching, don't you think?"

"No, Scott, I don't think that. Not at all. I'm telling you something is in this house." Ellen said emphatically.

Damn her husband and his close-mindedness. Ellen blamed his mother. Though Ellen liked the woman for the most part, Katherine Christianson was a devout Catholic who had little tolerance for paranormal beliefs. Clearly she had passed this opinion onto her son even though Scott himself was no longer a practicing Catholic.

"What do you say we take Natalie hiking at the park today?" Her husband asked, obviously wanting to drop their previous discussion.

Though Ellen knew she needed to spend some time doing normal things with her family, she desperately wanted to try to find Jenny's grandparents. Detective Crawley had said they lived in the area and Ellen wanted the opportunity to talk to them about their missing granddaughter.

"Actually, Scott, I've made plans with Marcie for the afternoon. She and I are going shopping." Ellen told her husband, though it wasn't true. Marcie, in fact, was spending the day with her two cousins, but Ellen needed an excuse to bail out on her family.

"I see. Well, then, I guess it'll just be Natalie and me." Scott said, clearly annoyed with his wife.

Ellen felt guilty. Surely she could find time to go to the park and also talk to Jenny's grandparents. "Well, I suppose if get a move on, I could make it back in time to meet up with Marcie. The mall is open until 6:00."

A smile brightened Scott's face. "Great! I'll go get Natalie dressed.

....

"That was so much fun!" Natalie exclaimed once they had returned home from the park.

"I know. It was fun." Ellen replied, smiling.

Though her mind had been occupied most of the drive to the park, she had forgotten her troubles once they were on the wooded trail. The weather had been perfect and the scenery beautiful. After they had finished their walk, the family had stopped for ice cream.

"What time are you supposed to meet Marcie?" Scott asked.

"Um, I have to call her and find out." Ellen answered, another twinge of guilt hitting her. She didn't like to lie, but Scott clearly wouldn't understand the purpose of her visit to Jenny's grandparents.

She made a show of going into the kitchen and using the phone. She actually spent the time on the phone checking her bank account balance, all the while talking as if Marcie were on the other line.

"Ok. See you soon." Ellen said loud enough for Scott to hear from the other room.

Walking into the living room where Scott and Natalie had planted themselves on the couch to watch the Disney channel, Ellen announced that she and Marcie were just going to meet at the mall in a half-hour. After that, she headed upstairs to change her clothes and freshen up her hair and make-up.

Before she walked out the door, she stopped to kiss both Scott and Natalie. "Bye, guys! I'll be home in a few hours."

"Ok. See you later, hon." Scott said.

Once in the car, Ellen drove down the road a bit and then pulled over. Before she could talk to Jenny's grandparents, she had to find out where they lived. She figured she could do a name search on the county auditor's website to get the information she needed.

After ten minutes of research, Ellen found what she was looking for. As it turned out, Jenny's grandparents, the McGreggors, lived only a few minutes from the town library on a street named Rolling Meadows. Ellen put the car back in drive and headed that way.

The house was located on a quiet, tree-lined street three blocks from the library. It was a yellow cape-cod with white trim and beautiful landscaping. There was an older gentleman trimming the rose bushes that lined the side of the garage, a small well-groomed toy poodle sitting by his side.

Ellen called out from the driveway, "Mr. McGreggor?"

The older man glanced up from his chore. "Yes. Can I help you?"

"I was wondering if I could possibly speak with you and your wife. My name is Ellen Christianson and I live over on Owl Creek drive. It's about your granddaughter." Ellen said.

"My wife died last year. It's just me now. Which granddaughter?" Mr. McGreggor inquired.

"Jenny." Ellen told him.

The old man seemed to consider this as he stood up, wiping his hands on his jeans. "Who are you again?"

"Mr. McGreggor, I know this is a bit unusual, but I really don't know what else to do. My family's life might be in danger. I have to find out about Jenny and the day she disappeared." Ellen pleaded.

Perhaps it was the look of sheer desperation on her face that swayed the old man to talk to her.

"Please call me Jim. We can talk on the porch. Would you care for some lemonade?" He offered as he walked to the porch and took a seat in one of two white rocking chairs.

"No, thank you. Mr. McGreggor- sorry, Jim- what can you tell me about the night Jenny disappeared?" Ellen asked taking a seat in the

other rocker. The little poodle promptly
curled up by her feet.

"Let's see. It was a long time ago, you
understand?" He said.

Ellen nodded.

"Well, Jenny was staying with us for the
summer. Her parents are both biologists and
had an opportunity to work off the coast of
Florida, so they had Jenny come stay with us.
We were delighted. Jenny was an angel just like
her mother always was. Anyway, while she was
here, she made friends with some kids in the
neighborhood and they asked her to go to the
library with them. It seemed harmless. The
library isn't far from here, you know?"

Ellen knew. She nodded at the older
man to continue.

"I don't think her mother ever forgave
us. I mean, she still calls from time to time, but
it isn't like before Jenny disappeared. We used
to always get together for the holidays and the
grandkids-Jenny has a younger brother and
sister-would stay weekends. It all stopped after
Jenny disappeared." Jim told her.

"I'm so sorry to hear that." Ellen said.
"What do you think happened to Jenny?"

"If you don't mind my asking, why do
you want to know about Jenny?" He asked.

It was a question Ellen had been
anticipating. She had prepared a rational

answer. For some reason, however, she broke down. Maybe it was the stress of all that had happened to her, but at that moment, in front of a man she had just met, Ellen cried almost uncontrollably. To his credit, Jim McGreggor said nothing. He didn't mock her or ask her what the hell was wrong with her. Instead, he just sat there quietly listening until she regained her composure.

"Ms. Christianson, are you okay?" he asked gently, offering her a handkerchief.

"Oh, I'm so sorry. I don't know what came over me. I'm just so…scared. I don't know how to say this without sounding like a nutcase, but Jenny's ghost is in my house. I know this sounds crazy, but it's true. I've seen her." Ellen said, as a thought suddenly occurred to her. "Did Detective Crawley give you the locket I found?"

"No. What locket?" the older man asked, clearly confused.

"I found a locket in my basement, hidden behind one of the foundation stones. I took it to the police department and talked to Detective Crawley. He told me the picture in the locket was of Jenny. You haven't heard from him?"

"No one has contacted me in years about Jenny. I remember that detective though. He worked on the case when Jenny disappeared.

He used to call or stop by often to update us on the case. Eventually, he stopped calling or stopping over. I guess he was tired of always delivering bad news.

"I always believed Jenny was dead. She never would've just taken off. She was a good girl. Happy. Smart too. She wanted to be a journalist when she grew up. And she could've done it. That girl had integrity. Always believed in doing the right thing. God, I miss her." He said, his voice choking up.

"I think that whoever killed Jenny may have killed another girl too. Emily Garritson. Do you recognize her name?"

Ellen watched as the old man's brow furrowed in concentration.

"Garritson, you say? I do remember that name, but not Emily. It was a boy. He went to the library that night with Jenny and the others. I can't remember his name, though."

"Eric?" Ellen asked quietly.

"Maybe. Yeah, I think that was it. Eric. Was he related to this Emily girl?"

"Her brother. Eric was Emily's brother."

Chapter 17

Driving home, Ellen could hardly believe what she had learned. This new information was the first connection she had between Emily and Jenny. But what did it mean? Also, why hadn't Detective Crawley returned the locket?

The sudden honking of a horn brought Ellen's focus back to the road. Not paying attention, she had crossed the double yellow line and nearly side swiped another vehicle. She jerked the steering wheel to the right and brought the car back into her lane. She let out a shaky breath.

So, Jenny had known Eric Garritson. Not only that, but he had also been with her the last time she had been seen. But was he connected to her disappearance? And if so, how? Eric would've been roughly the same age as Jenny, so it wouldn't be far-fetched that they could have met. They easily could've met through mutual friends or at some of the local hangouts.

Somehow, Ellen knew she had to find out how all of these events were connected-and soon.

....

Later that evening, Ellen called her boss at home and explained that she was going to need to take an unexpected week of vacation time. She attempted to fumble through a far-fetched explanation of how her basement had flooded due to a water main break and she was going to have to be at home to help with the clean up. Her boss told her not to worry about it. She thanked him and hung up.

"Who were you talking to, honey?" Scott asked from behind her.

"Oh, um...my boss." Ellen answered. "I've requested some vacation time for this week."

"Ok, but why? We usually use our vacation time to go to camping."

"I know, Scott, but I really need some time off. I'm just so stressed about all that's been happening with the house. And besides, I can get some things done around here while I'm off." Ellen told him.

"Sure. Ok. What do you want for dinner?" He asked, clearly annoyed and trying to cover it up.

Well, let him be annoyed, Ellen thought. He had been far from supportive in this whole matter and she didn't feel like explaining to him her real plans for the upcoming week.

"Whatever you want." She answered.

"Cheryl from work gave me a new recipe for chicken curry. Maybe I could try to make that?"

"That sounds wonderful. Do you need me to do anything?"

"No. Just go hang out with Natalie. I'll call you when it's ready." He said, already rummaging in the cabinet for a pot.

Ellen made her way into the living room where her daughter was nestled on the couch, an afghan covering her tiny body.

"Whatcha doing?" Ellen asked, taking a seat by her daughter's feet.

"Watching Spongebob. Patrick got a new nose!" she exclaimed happily.

"Cool. Mind if I watch with you?"

"Ok. You can lay down with me if you want." The little girl said.

Ellen smiled and crawled behind her daughter, wrapping her arms around the child. It felt good and before long, they were both absorbed in all the latest happenings in Bikini Bottom.

After a while, Ellen began to feel drowsy. Her eyelids were growing heavier by the minute. She shifted positions in an attempt to thwart off sleep, but she was too drained and eventually she gave in and closed her eyes.

Sleep was just taking hold of her when Natalie said in a whisper, "Mommy?"

"Hmmm…?" Ellen answered drowsily, her eyes still closed.

"She says it's really cold and dark where she's at." The little girl stated.

"Who, baby?" Ellen asked, thinking Natalie was talking about the show.

"Jenny."

At this, Ellen bolted upright, her mind suddenly clear and focused. "What do you mean, Natalie?"

"She's in the lake, mommy. And she wants out." Natalie answered, clearly unaware of the panic that was seizing her mother.

"Who told you that?" Ellen demanded.

"She did, mommy. She says she needs our help to get her out of the lake!" Natalie said, her voice raising an octave.

Ellen's mind raced. Jenny had been talking to Natalie? What did she mean about the lake? A horrible thought suddenly occurred to Ellen; Jenny's body was in the lake. It made sense. It would explain why all of this was happening. Ellen knew what she had to do.

"Scott!" Ellen yelled for her husband. "Scott, get in here!"

"What is it?" Scott asked as he ran into the living room, wiping his hands on a dish towel.

"Scott, call the police! She's in the lake. Jenny's body is in the lake!" Ellen wailed.

"Ellen, what are you talking about?" Scott demanded, clearly confused.

Ellen didn't answer him. She raced to the kitchen where she had left her cell phone. She punched in 911 and explained to the operator that she needed the police right away. She told the woman on the other end of the line that there was a body in her lake and then hung up.

....

"So, tell me again, Mrs. Christianson, what makes you think the body of Jenny Matthews is in your lake?" the police officer asked.

Ellen sighed. She had been over this already. How many times did she have to tell this man what had happened?

"I was sitting on the couch with my daughter when she told me that there was a girl's body in our lake." Ellen told him.

He looked at her expectantly.

"At that point, I called 911." Ellen continued.

"Uh-huh. And just what makes you so certain it's Jenny Matthews?" the officer inquired.

Ellen knew he was just doing his job, but she had already told him everything. She could tell by the way he looked at her that he didn't believe her. She didn't care. All that was important was he had taken her seriously enough to call in a diver and forensics team. At the moment, with just a few minutes of daylight remaining, the diver was in the lake searching.

"Here honey." Scott said, handing her a cup of hot coffee, and putting his arm around her shoulders.

Despite the obvious shock he had suffered, Scott had remained by her side. He had insisted to police that neither his wife nor his daughter would make something like this up.

"Hey Gary! Get over here!" One of the other officers called from the lake.

Officer Kolby turned to Ellen and Scott, "You just stay right here. I'll be right back."

Ellen turned to Scott. "Do you think I'm crazy?"

"No, sweetie. I just don't understand how Natalie could've seen a body in the lake. I mean, the diver has been in the water for almost 20 minutes and hasn't turned up anything. Are you sure she didn't just dream about it?" Scott asked.

Before she could answer, Ellen was interrupted by a fury of activity on the lake's edge. She could see that the diver was out of the water. He and two other men were pulling on a cable that was submerged in the water.

Just then, they hoisted something attached to the cable out of the water.

Ellen took off running. Regardless of Officer Kolby's warnings, she had to see for herself what they had found.

"Mrs. Christianson, please stay back." One of the officers told her.

"This is my property. You can't tell me what to do." Ellen said, pushing her way past him.

On the grassy slope a few feet from the lake's edge, Ellen could see what appeared to be a bundle of some kind. It looked like a large blue comforter with duct tape wrapped around it in three places. The duct tape had come loose at one end and Ellen could clearly make out the skeletal remains of a human foot.

"Dear God!" she exclaimed.

"Is that what I think it is?" A deep voice asked from behind Ellen.

Turning, she saw Detective Crawley, hands on hips, staring at the bundle. The officers on scene had called him in because of his association with the Jenny Matthews case.

"Hey, Don. We just pulled it up from the lake. It looks like a body." Officer Kolby explained to the detective. "Mrs. Christianson thinks it's Jenny Matthews."

"I see. Mrs. Christianson, could you and your husband please go inside now? This is official police business. I'll be in shortly to talk to you." Don Crawley said. "And Jake, you need to secure this crime scene. And call the coroner."

Ellen allowed Scott to usher her to the house. She really couldn't bear to see anymore, so she didn't put up a fight. She was certain, without any doubt, that the body the police had pulled from the lake was indeed Jenny Matthews.

Chapter 18

The next morning, Ellen slept until almost 9:00. Scott had taken Natalie to his parents' house the night before while Ellen remained behind and answered all of the police's questions. It had been well after midnight before she crawled into bed, too exhausted to let the night's events ward off sleep.

When she ventured downstairs, she could smell coffee and bacon. Scott was in the kitchen preparing breakfast.

"I made bacon, eggs, and toast. And coffee, of course. Is that ok?" he asked.

Ellen nodded, reaching for a mug and then pouring herself a cup of coffee. Normally she would add cream and sugar, but this morning she drank it black, savoring the strong taste.

"Did you sleep well?" Scott asked, as he dipped up scrambled eggs from a skillet.

"Actually, I slept better last night than I have for weeks." She told him, accepting the plate of food he offered.

Sitting down at the table, she found her appetite was monstrous and she immediately began to devour her eggs.

"Do you want to talk about it?" Scott asked.

"I'm just glad it's over, Scott. I know you think I've been out of my mind these last few weeks, but I knew something was in this house. It was Jenny. She wanted her body found. Wanted a decent burial. Now she can have peace." Ellen said, pushing her near empty plate away.

Taking her hand, Scott stared into his wife's eyes, "Ellen, I know I was skeptical. Hell, I still am, but I believe you sensed something. You and Natalie both. It's going to take me a while to wrap my brain around all of it, but I want you to know I love you and I'll never doubt you again. Okay?"

"Okay. I love you too. I think we can finally put all this behind us and get on with our lives now. By the way, a few days ago, I asked Father Donovan to stop by and bless the house. I can cancel if you want, but I don't see the harm in it. I think it will help us make a fresh start." Ellen said.

"Sure. I agree. What time is he supposed to be here?" Scott asked.

"At eleven. That gives us plenty of time to shower and clean up these dirty dishes." Ellen said.

"Sounds good. You go get in the shower and I'll do the dishes. Deal?" he asked.

"Deal." She told him.

....

Twenty minutes later, Ellen finished toweling off her hair. The bathroom was full of steam and she used her hand to wipe the mirror above the sink. Her reflection stared back at her. Tired. She looked tired. But she felt better. She felt as though this whole ordeal was over. Grabbing her hairbrush, she headed to the bedroom to put on clean clothes.

As she finished dressing herself in jeans and a black tank top, she heard Scott calling from downstairs. Casting a quick glance in the mirror, she made her way downstairs, running the brush through her hair as she went.

"What is it?" she asked when she reached the kitchen.

"Detective Crawley called. They positively identified the body as Jenny Matthews. Apparently they matched the dental records. Thought you'd want to know." He finished telling her.

Ellen let out a deep breath. Of course, this information was what she'd expected, had known in her heart, but she still felt a deep sense of sadness at the confirmation. Over the past couple of months, she felt like she had gotten to know Jenny. It was terribly upsetting news.

"You ok?" Scott asked tenderly.

"Yeah. I mean I knew it already. It just seems like such a waste, you know? She was so young." Ellen told her husband.

"I know what you mean. Detective Crawley said they may not be able to determine cause of death due to the body being skeletal. He said they're going to call in a forensic anthropologist to look at the bones, see if there's any identifiable marks on them that would help establish cause of death." Scott said.

"She was strangled." She said matter-of-factly.

Scott looked at her for a moment before saying anything. "Well, I guess we may never know for sure."

"I think I'm going to take a walk. Clear my head before Father Donovan gets here. Wanna join me?" she asked.

"Sure. Just let me go grab my tennis shoes." He told her.

....

Father Donovan arrived promptly at 11:00 with Danielle in tow. The younger woman was looking as lovely as Ellen remembered, wearing a cream and yellow sundress and white sandals. Her hair hung loosely around her shoulders and shone in the sunlight.

Father Donovan was dressed in jeans and a short-sleeved button up shirt, but he still wore his collar, the only affirmation in his dress that suggested he was a priest.

"Ellen, good to see you!" he said as he took her hand and smiled.

"Father Donovan, I'd like for you to meet my husband, Scott." Ellen said.

"Pleased to meet you, Father." Scott told the man as he shook his hand.

Ellen invited the two inside and offered them something to drink. Danielle asked for a diet coke. Father Donovan declined. Ellen showed them into the kitchen where they could talk before the blessing began.

"Father Donovan-"Ellen began.

"Please call me Jerry." He politely interrupted.

"Um, ok. Jerry, so much has happened since we last talked. I don't even know where to begin…" Ellen said, her voice trailing off.

"What Ellen means is, well, the police found the body of a girl that disappeared some time ago in our lake last night." Scott said.

Danielle gasped out loud at this latest information.

"Wow. That's terrible. I'm so sorry you had to go through that." Jerry Donovan said meaningfully, his brow furrowed with concern.

"It was the body of the girl I told you about when we last met. Jenny Matthews." Ellen stated.

"That's incredible. She's been missing for so long. How did the police find her?" he asked.

"My daughter, Natalie, found her. She claims that Jenny's spirit told her." Ellen said, again feeling slightly foolish discussing the nature of Jenny's body being found.

"Well, Ellen, that's awful. Is Natalie ok?" Danielle inquired.

"She's fine. She's staying at Scott's parents' house for a few days. Just until things blow over." Ellen explained.

"But you still want to proceed with the blessing?" Jerry asked.

"Yes. Scott and I feel that it will help put an end to all this so we can start fresh." Ellen told him.

She neglected to mention the blessing she and Marcie had performed on the house. She really didn't want to startle him. Besides, she honestly believed Jenny could finally move on now that her body would be given a proper burial.

"Very well." Jerry said. "I'll get started then. Danielle can remain here with you and explain the process, but it's really pretty basic."

"Thanks, Father." Scott and Ellen said in unison.

While they waited, Danielle talked with them about the church and how she'd come to work there. She claimed that she couldn't imagine a better job or a better boss. According to her, Father Donovan was a devoted priest and a decent man. Ellen got the impression that Danielle might have developed a crush on him.

"So, are you originally from this area?" Ellen asked her.

"Actually, I grew up in Georgia, but moved here in my late teens. My father was an engineer and we moved up here when his company relocated. I really do love it here though." She told them.

As they continued to talk, Ellen found herself really liking Danielle. Not only was she beautiful on the outside, but she was a genuinely sweet woman with a quick wit. Before she knew it, Father Donovan had finished the blessing.

"Well, I think we're all finished here." He said.

Danielle stood up and Ellen realized they were ready to leave. "Thank you so much for coming, Father. This really means a lot to us."

"Not a problem, my child. It's what I do." He smiled brightly at her.

With Scott beside her, she walked them to the door. They spent a few more moments exchanging pleasantries and then the two left. Ellen closed the door behind them and let out a sigh of relief.

"Glad it's over?" Scott asked.

"Yeah. I am. The house almost feels cleaner, don't you think?" she asked him.

"I guess it does. Now, what say we relax on the couch the rest of the day? We can eat junk food and watch those corny chick flicks you like."

Ellen playfully punched him in the arm. "They're not corny!"

"Whatever you say. Go pull something up on Netflix and I'll grab the chips and dip." Scott told her as he walked towards the kitchen.

Yes, Ellen thought happily. Things are finally getting back to normal.

Chapter 19

The next few days passed with marvelous monotony. Ellen, Scott, and Natalie would share breakfast, laughing and talking about the upcoming weekend. Then, Scott would head off to work, leaving Ellen and Natalie home to do as they pleased.

Since Ellen decided not to return to work until her scheduled vacation had expired, it left plenty of time for her to get things done around the house. She and Natalie would do housework and run errands in the morning, then retire to the park for a walk or to climb on the jungle gym. In the late afternoon, Natalie would watch television or play in her room while Ellen prepared dinner in time for Scott's arrival home.

On one such evening, Ellen had just finished grilling steaks. She heard Scott's car in the driveway and hurried inside with the steaks. She had set the table before starting on the steaks, so she placed the plate of steaks in the center of the table and called for Natalie. "Sweetie, dinner's ready!"

Scott waltzed through the front door, tossing his keys on the entry table. "Hey, sweetheart."

"How was your day?" Ellen asked as she pulled the baked potatoes out of the oven.

"Oh, the usual. Long. Tiring. In general, hellish. But I'm home now and tomorrow's Friday." He told her, putting his hands on her waist and kissing her gently.

"Mmmm. Yummy." Ellen murmured.

Releasing her, Scott sat down at the table. "Everything looks delicious. I've got to tell you, I'm starving. I had to skip lunch. Where's Natalie?"

"I've already called her. She's playing in her room." Ellen said absently as she grabbed a bottle of wine. "Is Merlot ok?

"That's perfect. Call Natalie again, will ya?" he asked, "If I don't eat soon, I think my stomach may devour itself."

"Natalie! Come on down here! Your food is getting cold!" Ellen yelled as she prepared her daughter's plate, carefully cutting the steak into tiny little pieces the way Natalie liked.

After several moments, there was still no response from upstairs, so Ellen pried herself up from her chair and ran upstairs. When she arrived at the top, she saw that Natalie's door was closed. She placed her hand on the knob and called her daughter's name again as she turned the knob. It was locked.

"Natalie, unlock the door." Ellen said.

On the other side of the door, Ellen could hear Natalie's voice. It sounded as though she was talking to someone.

"Natalie, do you hear me? Open the door!" she called out again.

There was no response from the child. She just continued talking away, ignoring her mother.

"This isn't funny. Open the door now!" Ellen yelled, her patience growing thin.

Again, Natalie ignored her.

"Scott, could you come here please?" Ellen called down the stairs to her husband.

Moments later, Scott was beside her at Natalie's door. "What is it?"

"She won't open the door and it's locked." Ellen explained, again twisting the knob and knocking on the door.

"Natalie, open the door." Scott said.

A few seconds passed.

"Natalie, open the door now or you're not going swimming at grandma's this weekend." Scott said.

"She's not listening. I don't know what's gotten into her." Ellen said genuinely perplexed by her daughter's behavior.

"Who in the hell is she talking to?" Scott demanded.

"I don't know. She's been talking this whole time. I can't make out what she's saying though."

"Well, that does it!" Scott said, anger fringing his words. "I'm going to get the key."

Ellen watched as Scott ran down the stairs, his socked feet thudding softly on the stairs as he descended. Within moments, he returned, key in hand. Placing the key in the lock, he turned it and opened the door.

Natalie sat in the middle of the floor on her braided oval rug. Toys lay scattered all around her. She didn't look up when they entered. In fact, she didn't appear to notice them at all.

"Natalie, didn't you hear me?" Ellen asked.

The child continued to talk quietly to herself, seemingly oblivious to her mother's question.

"Natalie, answer your mother!" Scott yelled.

When the child again refused to acknowledge them, Ellen was unsure what to do. Natalie was staring straight ahead, her eyes glazed, fixed on something directly in front of her. Only there was nothing there. She continued to talk as though having a conversation with a friend.

Ellen reached down and grabbed her arm. The sudden action seemed to jar Natalie out of her trance. Her eyes focused and she seemed confused.

"What is wrong with you? I've been calling you for ten minutes." Ellen said.

"I'm sorry mommy. I was playing and I didn't hear you." Natalie told her.

"Who were you talking to?" Ellen demanded.

"Don't be mad, mommy. I was talking to Jenny." The child said her voice choking up as tears began to stream down her face.

Shock hit Ellen like a sledgehammer in the chest. She could hardly breathe and the room began to spin. She felt Scott take hold of her and sit her on the bed.

Finally, regaining her voice, she said, "But Jenny's gone, Natalie."

The child looked at her. Her voice quivered. "No, she isn't, mommy. She's sitting right next to you."

Without thinking, Ellen grabbed Natalie and pulled her from the room, Scott right on her heels. The three of them fled downstairs. Ellen didn't say another word. She simply sat down at the dining room table and began eating her steak. Though her hunger and completely dissipated, she needed to do something. Anything.

From across the table, her eyes met Scott's. For the first time since all of this began, Ellen saw something new in her husband's expression. Fear.

....

"What are we going to do?" Ellen asked her husband hopelessly.

It was well past 11:00pm and they were seated on their bed. Scott had dragged Natalie's mattress into their room and the child lay sleeping peacefully, her arms wrapped around Boo.

"Shit, I don't know." Scott said, running his fingers through his hair, a glass of bourbon in his other hand.

"We found her body. I thought for sure that's what she wanted. Now, I don't know." Ellen said.

"We just have to try to remain positive, honey. Maybe she just wanted to say goodbye to Natalie." Scott suggested.

Ellen didn't believe that. Why was Jenny focusing her attention on Natalie? Since her body had been discovered in the lake, Ellen hadn't had any bizarre experiences. She hadn't even *felt* anything. It was clear, though, that Jenny was still in the house. And communicating with Natalie. But why?

"I just don't know what else to do. I mean, I tried to ask Natalie what Jenny said to her, but she said she really didn't remember. And she did appear to be in some kind of…trance when we went into her room. But what does it all mean? I'm really scared, Scott." Ellen said, tears spilling onto her cheeks.

"It'll be ok." Scott told her as he sat his empty glass on the nightstand and wrapped his arms around her.

"But what if it isn't? What if Jenny does something to Natalie? She obviously wants something. I just don't know what. Why did any of this ever have to happen?" Ellen asked.

"I honestly don't know, sweetie. But everything happens for a reason, right? We just have to figure out what that reason is." Scott told his wife.

"I'm going to talk to Eric Garritson tomorrow." Ellen said.

"What? Why?" Scott asked.

"Because I spoke to Jenny's grandfather, and he told me that Eric was with Jenny the night she disappeared. It's all I have to go on. Maybe he can shed some light onto what happened to her. Maybe that's what she wants; for everyone to know what happened to her." Ellen told him.

"You have to be careful, Ellen. I don't think you should go alone. Maybe I can get off work tomorrow and go with you." He suggested.

"No. I called Marcie earlier. She's going to meet me at Natalie's daycare in the morning and we're going to drive out there together. I'll be fine." She said.

"Okay. But call me as soon as you leave and let me know what he says. Now, let's try to get some sleep." Scott said.

Chapter 20

The next morning, Ellen dropped Natalie off at the daycare then waited in the parking lot for Marcie. Earlier she had looked up Eric Garritson's address in the directory. It was about a 20-minute drive from the daycare.

Just then, Marcie pulled up in her black Jeep Wrangler. She pulled into the space next to Ellen and then hopped out.

"We taking your car?" she asked Ellen.

"That's fine." Ellen told her.

"Okay. Just let me grab some stuff from my car." Marcie said.

Ellen watched as Marcie rummaged around in her vehicle, grabbing her purse and two Styrofoam cups of coffee. Then she locked the doors and climbed into Ellen's car.

"Did you get the address?" she asked once she was buckled in.

"Yeah. It's in Beavercreek on a street called Dunhaven. It's directly off Rt. 42." Ellen told her as she put the car in gear.

"How's Natalie?" Marcie asked, as she handed Ellen one of the coffees.

"She's okay, I guess." Ellen said as she gratefully took a sip of the coffee. "It's weird. She doesn't seem to remember what she and Jenny talked about. What really bothers me is she doesn't appear to be scared. I mean, wouldn't you freak out if a ghost of someone who's been dead for over 20 years was chatting you up?" Ellen asked her friend.

"Hell yeah. But kids are so resilient. And she's so young. She probably doesn't think it's bizarre." Marcie said.

"I also called Detective Crawley this morning. They don't have any new information on Jenny's death, but they are going to be re-interviewing everyone that was with Jenny that night. When I asked him about Eric, he said he was unaware that he had known Jenny, let alone had been with her the night she disappeared." Ellen said.

"Hmmm. That's interesting. Why do you think the grandparents never mentioned it to the police?" Marcie inquired.

"They probably forgot. The grandfather didn't remember Eric until I brought up Emily's name." Ellen said.

Marcie seemed to contemplate this. "Do you think he could've killed Jenny?"

"Eric? I don't know. I doubt it. He was just a kid at the time. Besides, I met him. He didn't seem like a killer. What I don't understand is why the police didn't connect Jenny's disappearance with Emily Garritson's murder. I mean, they happened just a few years apart." Ellen said.

"Well, that's true, but the police thought Emily was killed by that other guy…Morten whatever his name was." Marcie said.

"Sullivan. It was Morten Sullivan. But I'm positive he didn't do it. I don't know why I believe that, but I do. Someone clearly went to a lot of trouble to frame him though." Ellen concluded.

They drove in silence for the rest of the way, admiring the scenery as they passed. The day was beautiful with blue skies and white fluffy clouds. Ellen had the windows down, and the sweet smell of summer filled the car.

Beavercreek was a relatively new neighborhood, the area once consisting of farms. A few years back, a land developer bought up the land and began building. There was now a huge mall, several upscale eateries, and a country club equipped with a beautiful golf course. Eric Garritson's house was just a few minutes from the country club, his rear yard backing up to the golf course.

"Wow. That's a nice house." Marcie remarked as they pulled into the driveway.

Ellen regarded the house. It was nice. And big. The front yard was lush with green, closely mown grass and tasteful landscaping. The house itself was a grayish white brick with huge windows and two tall pillars that reached to the top story. A black Mercedes SUV was parked in the drive and a small white dog was milling about the lawn, an electronic collar around its neck.

"Do you think he bites?" Marcie asked.

"I'm willing to take my chances." Ellen said as she climbed out of the car.

Though the little dog barked furiously, once it was within a few feet of the women, it began jumping up and down excitedly. Ellen stuck out her hand and let the dog sniff it. In return, the dog feverishly licked her outstretched fingers. "I don't think we have anything to worry about." Ellen told her friend with a smile.

They made their way to the massive double front doors. Ringing the doorbell, they waited. The little dog circled their legs, occasionally stopping to sniff. At one point, it hiked its leg on one of the two potted plants on the porch.

The door suddenly opened and a pretty blonde woman wearing a pink robe looked out at them. "Can I help you?"

Ellen reached out her hand and introduced herself and Marcie. Meanwhile, the dog hiked its leg again, this time on one of the pillars.

"Winston! Get in here!" The woman yelled at the dog.

Winston cocked his head to the side and regarded her for a moment before making a beeline to the yard.

"That dog doesn't listen whatsoever!" The woman exclaimed.

"He's really cute, though." Marcie said.

"Hmph. My husband's idea of a birthday gift." She said. "I would much rather have had jewelry or perfume. What do you want?"

Talk about getting right to the point.

"Actually, we wanted to speak to your husband if he's here. He used to live in the house I bought and I had some questions about its history." Ellen told her.

"He already left for work." She said flatly.

"Oh. We were really hoping to speak with him today. It's somewhat important." Ellen said, hoping the woman would reveal his whereabouts.

No such luck.

"I'm sorry, but he won't be home until around 6:00pm. Leave your number and I'll have him call you." She said.

Ellen jotted down her number on a slip of paper from her purse and handed it to the woman. She folded the paper and stuffed it into the pocket of her robe. "I'll have him call you."

She repeated then shut the door without so much as a goodbye.

Back in the car Marcie said, "What a bitch."

"Marcie! You don't even know her." Ellen reprimanded her friend.

"Maybe not but she was totally rude. And that poor dog! I don't blame him for not listening to her."

Ellen couldn't disagree. The woman had been rude. But at least she'd taken her number. Maybe Eric would call and she could find out his relationship with Jenny. Hopefully he would be more helpful than his wife.

....

Two days passed with no word from Eric. Ellen was growing more and more frustrated by the minute. She needed to figure out where he worked so she could maybe catch him there. But she didn't even know what *kind* of work he did, let alone where.

A sudden idea occurred to Ellen. The Fischers had known Eric and Noreen had mentioned that Eric had gone to college. Perhaps she would have some idea where he worked. Ellen snatched up her cell phone.

"Hello." Said a male voice.

"Stanley? Hi, it's Ellen Christianson. Is Noreen around?" she said into the phone.

"Uh, yeah, Ellen. Hold on a sec. Let me see if I can pry her away from whatever shopping channel she's watching." He said.

Ellen could hear him yelling for his wife to get the phone. Within seconds she heard an audible click as another line was picked up.

"I've got it, Stanley." Noreen said into the phone.

As Stanley hung up, Ellen dove right in. "Noreen, hi, it's Ellen. How are you?"

"Oh, Ellen. Hi. I'm well. And yourself?" Noreen asked politely.

"I'm good, Noreen. Listen, I just have a quick question I was hoping you could answer. I'm still trying to find some history on my house and I'm trying to get in touch with Eric Garritson. Do you by chance know where he works?" she asked.

"Well, I'm not quite sure, dear. I know he's a lawyer. I think Gale mentioned his employer once or twice, but it's slipping my mind. Oh, but I do remember it's close to where he lives." She said excitedly.

"Thanks, Noreen. Do you know what kind of attorney he is?" Ellen asked.

"Um, let's see. Something to do with estates maybe. Or taxes. Or something like that." Noreen answered.

"Wow. That's helpful. I'm sure I can find him. I have to go now, but maybe we could get together later this week. Have dinner perhaps." Ellen told the woman.

"Oh, that sounds delightful." Noreen agreed and then her voice took on a conspiratorial tone. "I noticed the police cars at your house last week. Is everything okay?" she asked.

Ellen didn't want to be rude but she didn't have time to explain things at the moment. "I'll fill you in when we meet up for dinner okay?"

Begrudgingly Noreen agreed. Ellen said goodbye and hung up. She immediately called her boss at home. He answered on the second ring.

"Andrew, hi, it's Ellen. Sorry to bother you at home. Do you by chance know an estate attorney named Eric Garritson?" she asked.

"Garritson…yes I think he works at Luxworth and Hall. What's this about?" he asked.

"I'm just trying to do some research on my home. He's the son of the previous owner and I wanted to try to get hold of him. Thanks for the information, Andrew. I'll see you at work tomorrow!" Ellen said as cheerfully as she could.

Once she hung up, she grabbed her cell phone and Googled the law firm Andrew had mentioned. Scrolling through the search results, she located a website for Luxworth and Hall. She quickly found the phone number and started dialing. She glanced at the clock. Ten till 6:00pm. She wondered if anyone would still be at the office. It was worth trying.

The phone rang five times on the other end and Ellen was about to hang up when a woman's voice answered. "Luxworth and Hall. How can I help you?"

"Hi. I was wondering if Eric Garritson was still in?" she asked.

"I'm sorry, ma'am, but Mr. Garritson left work yesterday for a family emergency. He's not expected to return until Thursday. Is there something I can help you with? She asked politely.

"Um, no, thank you. I'll call back later this week." Ellen said then hung up.

Damn. A family emergency. Well, she supposed that explained why he hadn't phoned her. Now what? It would do her no good to talk to Jenny's grandfather again. She didn't think he had any more information about Eric.. Perhaps she could drop by the local high school in the morning before work and inquire about Eric. Somehow, she had to find out something. Fast.

Chapter 21

The next morning, Ellen was waiting patiently in the office at Crescentville High School. The principle, Lonnie Turner, was busy with morning announcements, so Ellen had been asked to take a seat until the woman was available.

The minutes ticked by slowly.

"Mrs. Christianson? Ms. Turner can see you now." The school aide working in the office told her.

Ellen walked down the hall to the left of the reception area into a small, cramped office. Though neat and orderly, it was stacked high with books and magazines. Lonnie Turner sat behind the metal desk. Approximately in her early sixties, she was a large-framed woman with short, curly gray hair. Her blue eyes were magnified behind thick glasses, and she wore a floral print blouse.

"Hi, Ms. Turner. My name is Ellen, and I was wondering if I could ask you a few questions about a student that used to go here." Ellen said.

Lonnie Turner stood up and shook Ellen's hand. "What kind of questions?"

Ellen had concocted a story that she hoped would prompt the woman to answer her questions but decided to go with the truth…for the most part.

"It's regarding Eric Garritson. He attended this high school a number of years ago." Ellen paused for effect. "I recently moved into the house he lived in as a teenager, and I was hoping to find out more about him. There are some…nuances about the house and I was hoping I could learn something that would help explain it.

"I see. Have you tried contacting him?" the principle asked.

Ellen nodded. "Yes. Several times. He won't return my phone calls. I don't want to bother him, but I thought if I could find out about him, about his past, it would help me explain some of the things about my house."

"Well, it's highly unusual for the school to release academic records for a student." Lonnie said.

"I don't want anything like that. I just want to know what kind of person he was. What kind of things he liked to do? Who his friends were? Things like that. Please." Ellen said, hoping her tone reflected desperation.

The woman seemed to consider this. "I remember Eric. I was a teacher back then and I had him in a few of my classes. He was bright, but…had trouble fitting in at times."

"So he didn't have any friends?"
Ellen asked. Perhaps if she could get the names
of some of his friends, she could ask them about
Jenny.

"For a while, he kept to himself mostly.
But then he started hanging out with a few
troubled boys." Lonnie told her.

"Troubled?" Ellen prompted.

"You know the type. Black clothes,
piercings, bad grades. Eric really wasn't
anything like them, so I don't know why they
became friends." Lonnie said.

"What about his adoptive sister, Emily?"
Ellen asked.

"They didn't seem close at all. Emily
was smart and dressed conservatively. She got
excellent grades. Pity what happened to her.
Once she died, though, Eric really changed for
the better. He stopped hanging out with those
delinquents, straightened out his grades, and
became more outgoing. Shame it took his
sister's death to provoke a change." Lonnie
sighed and shook her head slowly as if she had
seen this type of thing time and agian.

"Do you by chance remember the names
of any of his friends?" Ellen probed.

"Let's see…there was Josh Masters.
And Greg Lynn. A couple of others, but I don't
remember their names." She said.

"Thanks, Ms. Turner. You've been a big help." Ellen said standing up.

"You're more than welcome. You might also try to contact Elise Stanton. She was Eric's guidance counselor. She's retired now, but still lives in the area. I can call her if you'd like." The woman said.

"That would be wonderful. Thank you." Ellen said.

Lonnie Turner paged through a day planner and then picked up the phone. She greeted Elise Stanton warmly, explained the situation and then asked her if she would be available to meet with Ellen.

"Would this evening work for you?" she asked Ellen.

"Yes. I get off work around 5:00pm." Ellen told her.

Lonnie concluded the phone call and then said to Ellen, "She said 5:30 would be fine. Here's her address."

Ellen took the paper and placed it in her purse. "You've been very helpful, Ms. Turner. I can't thank you enough."

"Good luck, Ellen. And I hope Eric comes to his senses and takes your phone calls. I'm a huge advocate for the importance of family." The woman said.

Ellen agreed and then left the office. She had to hurry if she was to make it to work on time.

....

Elise Stanton lived in a small cottage nestled in the woods on the outskirts of town. The driveway was long and winding and well hidden by trees. Despite plugging the address into Google Maps, Ellen passed it up and drove another mile or so before she realized her mistake. The second time around, though, she found it and pulled in.

Elise was sitting in a weathered rocker on the small but cozy porch. The house was adorable and reminded Ellen of something out of Hansel & Gretel. As Ellen got out of her car and walked up to the porch she noticed hundreds of garden gnomes sitting about the yard.

Elise jumped up. "You must be Ellen! I just made lemonade. I hope you like it sweet!" the woman exclaimed. Though she was well into her seventies, the woman was spry. She was merrily bustling around the porch and busily pouring lemonade from a glass pitcher with hand-painted roses.

"And you must be Elise. It's nice to meet you." Ellen told the woman.

"You'll have to forgive me, dear. I don't get many visitors anymore and since my husband died, I get lonesome. Now, back in the day, I used to have some swinging parties!" she said with a wink.

Ellen laughed. The woman's cheerfulness was catching. Elise Stanton was thin and slightly bent over with wild gray hair that seemed to have a mind of its own. She wore bib overalls with a white Grateful Dead T-shirt underneath. It didn't appear that she was wearing a bra which seemed to fit with the free spirit vibe the older woman was putting out.

"Please, sit!" Elise told Ellen, indicating the other rocker.

Ellen sat down and took the lemonade Elise offered. "Thanks so much for seeing me. I know it's kind of last minute." She said, taking a sip of the lemonade. It was actually quite good.

"Pish posh." She said with a dismissive waive. "I love having company. And I love reminiscing about my students. You're Eric Garritson's sister, right?" she asked.

Again, Ellen felt a pang of guilt for lying, but it was the only way to get the information she needed without bringing up ghosts or dead bodies. "Yes. I just discovered he's my brother a few weeks ago. I've done a lot of research on the Internet, but I thought talking to people that knew him would be better."

"Well, you're in luck! I remember all my students. I may be old, but my mind's as sharp as a tack." Elise told her tapping her temple and offering another warm smile.

Ellen believed that. "What can you tell me about him? Ms. Turner said he fell in with the wrong crowd in high school." Ellen prompted.

"Oh, yes. I don't know what got into that boy. He was nothing like his sister, but these boys he hung around with were bad seeds. There were four of them. Greg Lynn, Derrick Miles, Josh Masters, and Eddie Lucas. I think they all had biology together. Greg ended up dropping out of school his junior year and Eddie's parents sent him away to some school further north. Only Eric, Derrick, and Josh graduated."

"What do you mean by 'bad seeds'?" Ellen asked.

"Constantly in trouble. Bad grades. Skipping school. You name it. Also, there were rumors among the other students about satanic worshiping." Elise said, her voice taking on a confidential tone.

"You mean they worshiped the devil?" Ellen asked, appalled.

Elise nodded emphatically. "Oh, yes. That's exactly what I mean. And it's true too. I once saw a pentagram on the front of Greg's math book. And they all dressed the part too. Dyed their hair black and always wore black clothes. And Josh had a tattoo of devil's horns on his upper back. Carrie Ellis told me she saw it one day after school when he had his shirt off." Elise told her.

Ellen considered this. "Was Eric involved?"

"At first, I think so, but after his sister was murdered, he cleaned up his act. I don't think I ever saw him with those boys again."

"That's good to know. What about the name Jenny Matthews? Does that mean anything to you?" Ellen asked.

"Hmmm…Jenny Matthews? You know, I think I remember Josh mentioning a girl by that name. Someone he met over the summer. She went missing, right?" Elise asked.

"Yes she did." Ellen said, barely listening.

"Do you know her too, dear?" Elise asked.

Ellen nodded. "Just a name I came across during my research."

"I don't want you to think Eric was all bad, because he wasn't. He just got in with the wrong crowd. It happens to the best of kids. He straightened out though." She pointed out.

"Yes he did. Do any of those boys still live around here?" Ellen asked.

"I know Josh does. He's a mechanic at Denver Automotive on Rt. 50. I took my car in there once for a tire rotation but right after I picked it up, it developed an oil leak and the brakes went out. Never went back. I haven't seen Eddie since high school. Derrick died in a drunk driving accident several years back and Greg is in prison. Armed robbery, I think." Elise said.

"Thanks, Elise. This information has been so helpful. I think I'm going to talk to Josh and see what he remembers about my brother." Ellen told her.

"Be careful, dear. That boy was the worst of the bunch if you ask me. And a tiger never changes its stripes, if you catch my drift." Elise warned.

"I'll be careful. So you live out here all by yourself?" Ellen asked, changing the subject. She sensed the Elisa was lonely and wanted to talk so she figured she could spare a few minutes and offer the woman some company.

They continued to talk for another half-hour. Ellen liked the woman and felt sorry for her. It had to be lonely living all by herself in the middle of the woods. When it was time for her to leave, she promised Elise that she wouldn't be a stranger. Elise surprised her with a warm hug. They parted ways and Ellen headed home.

....

"Satanism?" Marcie asked over the phone.

It was a little past 9:00pm that evening. Ellen had called her friend to fill her in on both her meeting with Lonnie Turner and Elise Stanton.

"Can you believe it? I think I'm onto something here, Marcie. Would you be available to meet with me tomorrow after work? I want to go talk to Josh Masters. See what he has to say." Ellen asked.

"I'm supposed to help my cousin design the website for the new business, but I think I can manage." Marcie said.

"Great. I'll swing by your apartment on my way home from work." Ellen told her.

They said goodnight and Ellen headed upstairs to bed. Hopefully, tomorrow would bring more answers than questions.

Chapter 22

"Are you sure this is the place?" Marcie asked.

The two women were sitting in Ellen's car outside of Denver Automotive. It was twenty past five and it was pouring down rain. According to the weatherman, it was going to rain until early morning. Ellen looked at the sky. Dark clouds were rolling overhead and thunder could be heard in the distance.

"This is the place Elise said Josh works. Come on. Let's go inside." Ellen said.

Together, they exited the car and ran towards the front door. Within seconds, both women were soaking wet. Ellen stepped into a puddle and water poured into her shoe.

"Shit!" she swore out loud.

Marcie reached the door first and swung it open, hurrying inside where it was dry. Ellen was close behind. The interior was small with beige walls and gray indoor/outdoor carpet. Four chairs and two small end tables sat to the right of the door and a wood, wraparound desk sat directly ahead. A small bathroom was tucked into the back corner next to a vending machine with a handwritten out-of-order signed taped to the front.

"Is it wet enough for ya?" the man behind the desk asked.

Ellen approached the desk and smiled. She noticed the man's name, which was sewed into his blue work shirt: Harvey. "Hi. I was wondering if Josh Masters was here?"

"Josh, huh? Did someone refer you?" he asked.

"Um, not exactly. This is a personal matter. I just need to talk to him for a few minutes." Ellen said sweetly.

"Yeah. He's out in the garage doing some brake work on some old lady's Buick. You the police?" he asked.

"No. Nothing like that. He's an old friend of someone I'm trying to get hold of." Ellen explained.

"Well you never know with Josh. Hold on. I'll go get him." Harvey said as he walked through the door that led to the garage.

A minute or so later, Harvey returned with another man, presumably Josh. He wore the same blue uniform as Harvey and was tall and lean. His coal black hair was slicked back and he had icy blue eyes. He may have been good-looking if not for the scowl he wore and the crescent shaped scar on his left cheek.

"These are the ladies that need to talk to you." Harvey told him.

Ellen extended her hand. "Hi. My name is Ellen and I was wondering if I could ask you a few questions about Eric Garritson?"

Josh looked contemplative for a moment and then said, "Eric, huh? I haven't talked to him in forever."

"Well, I've been trying to reach him, but he's out of town. I was wondering if you or Eric ever knew Jenny Matthews? She went missing several years ago." Ellen said.

Something flashed in Josh's eyes. Fear? Uncertainty? He quickly recovered and shook his head. "No. The name doesn't ring a bell. What's this about?"

"Hmmm. That's odd because I'm certain Jenny's grandfather said Jenny was with Eric the night she disappeared." Ellen told him.

"Look, lady, that's Eric's business. I ain't his keeper. I'm telling you I don't know her or anything about her going missing. Ok?" he said.

"Are you and Eric still friends?" Marcie asked, stepping up beside Ellen.

"No, blondie. Like I said, I haven't talked to him in years." Josh said, eyeing Marcie like a prime piece of meat displayed in the front window of a butcher's shop.

Undeterred, Marcie said, "Actually, my name is Marcie."

"Whatever." He said, turning his attention back to Ellen. "I suggest you talk to Eric. I don't have nothing else to say."

"Very well. Thanks for your time."
Ellen said.

As she and Marcie turned to leave, Josh
called out, "Hey, blondie! If you're over this
way again, look me up. Maybe we can go out."
Then he winked.

Marcie visibly shuddered then quickly
retreated out the door. Back in the car she said,
"What a total creep! I mean, ugh!"

"Yeah, he was kinda sleazy, huh? And I
got the distinct impression he was lying when I
asked about Jenny." Ellen said, starting the car.

"I thought so too. What next?" Marcie
asked.

"I don't know. Maybe I'll try Eric
again. He's due back to work tomorrow." Ellen
said.

"Well, in the meantime, can we stop and
get something to eat? I'm about to wither away
from hunger." Marcie said.

Ellen had to smile. It was amazing how
Marcie could eat and eat and still maintain a
perfect size 2 figure. "Yeah, we can stop
somewhere. Scott ordered pizza for him and
Natalie, so I don't have to worry about them.
What do you want?"

Marcie thought about it for a while.
"I'm really in the mood for something juicy and
delicious. How about Louie's?" Louie's was a

small barbecue restaurant not far from where they were.

"Sounds good. I could go for their beef brisket sandwich." Ellen said, her mouth already watering.

"Drizzled with their special sweet barbecue sauce?" Marcie asked.

"You know it." Ellen replied and headed east on Chester road.

····

That evening, Ellen put a call into Detective Crawley. She explained what she had discovered about Eric's connection to Jenny Matthews and the conversation she had with both Lonnie Turner and Elise Stanton. She then recounted her conversation with Josh Masters.

"So what are you saying?" Detective Crawley asked.

"Don't you think it's odd that Eric was with Jenny the night of her disappearance *and* I found her locket hidden in his childhood home?" Ellen wanted to know.

"Well, did you ask him about it? I mean, you've talked to everyone else it seems." The detective said, an obvious note of sarcasm dripping from his words.

Ellen couldn't believe it. Here she was doing his job and he thanked her by being a complete jackass. "Well, actually I've been trying to reach him but he's out of town. His office said he'd be back tomorrow. I was thinking maybe you could talk to him."

The detective sighed. "Mrs. Christianson, I assure you, my department is taking this matter very seriously, but there are certain protocols we have to follow. Also, I want you to stop snooping around. You don't have any business getting involved. This is a police matter and you need to quit waltzing around like Nancy Drew in the secret of the lost locket. It's dangerous. Furthermore, you could foul up this investigation."

"I wasn't aware there *was* an investigation. Maybe you don't think what I've learned is important, but I hope you at least consider it." Ellen said, her irritation rising with each word.

"I have written down everything you told me. I will look into it when I can. Not to sound callous, but there are more recent crimes I have to deal with. I will, however, do some research on this-"he broke off and Ellen could hear papers shuffling, "-Josh Masters fellow. I'll also look at Eric and see what I can find out. Will that make you happy?"

"I suppose so. Like it makes a difference anyway." Ellen said shortly.

"Ok. Can I do anything else for you?" he asked.

"No. You've been *very* helpful." Ellen said and then hung up.

The nerve of that man! How could he not see the relevance of Eric's obvious connection to Jenny? Or was she making something out of nothing? She didn't think so. There were just too many unanswered questions. And coincidences. Eric was with Jenny the night she disappeared. Jenny's locket had been hidden in Ellen's basement, presumably by Eric. Eric's sister was murdered just a few years after Jenny. Lastly, Eric had been a troubled teen who hung out with some unsavory friends who dabbled in the occult. It all suggested something sinister. The question was: who had killed Jenny and Emily?

....

The next day, Ellen left work shortly after 5:00pm. Traffic was worse than usual due to a three-car collision on Rt. 42. Ellen didn't get to Eric's office building until almost 5:40pm.

As she pulled into the lot, she noticed several cars still parked outside. Hopefully, one of them was Eric's. She parked her car, grabbed her purse and keys, and headed towards the entrance of the building.

Inside, she stepped into the entry. There was a brown leather sofa, a low coffee table with magazines, and several potted plants. Straight ahead was a directory with elevators flanking its sides. Ellen walked straight to the directory and looked for Eric's law firm. It was on the second floor in suite 220. She pressed the up arrow for the elevator and stepped back to wait. The doors opened immediately.

On the second floor, Ellen looked to her left and right. There was nothing to indicate which direction she should go, so she decided to head to the right. She was in luck. Suite 220 was the second door on the left. Ellen opened the door and stepped inside.

"May I help you?" a female voice greeted her immediately.

The voice came from behind a large mahogany desk directly in front of the door. The waiting area was small but cozy with leather wingback chairs and mahogany end tables. Ellen could hear classical music playing from tiny speakers in the corners of the room. Chopin, she thought. Ellen approached the desk.

"Hi. Is Eric Garritson in?" she asked.

"Do you have an appointment?" the receptionist asked. She was young; early 20's, with sleek shoulder-length black hair and olive skin. She wore a charcoal pantsuit that showed off a trim figure. She was pretty in an exotic way, but when she smiled, it didn't reach her large, brown eyes.

"I'm afraid I don't, but it's urgent I speak with him immediately. I've been trying to reach him for days, but he's been out of town. Can you please see if he's available?" Ellen asked.

"I'm sorry, but Mr. Garritson is very busy. You can schedule an appointment. I can get you in…next Wednesday around 2:00pm." She said, her eyes scanning over an appointment book on the desk in front of her.

"That won't work. Please tell him this is important. If he won't speak to me, I'll go to the police." Ellen said, trying to sound confident.

The woman stared at her, the expression on her face a mixture of irritation and disbelief. She sat there motionless for several seconds, unsure of what to do, and then finally reached for the phone. "Sorry to disturb you, Mr. Garritson, but there is a woman here *insisting* to speak with you." She paused, listening. "Ok. I'll tell her."

Turning to Ellen, she said, "If you'll have a seat, I'll call you when he's available."

"Thank you." Ellen said.

She took a seat in one of the chairs and picked up a *Vanity Fair* and began scanning the articles.

Ten minutes later, the receptionist told her that Mr. Garritson could see her now. She opened a door and told Ellen it was the third door on the right, then returned to her desk, not bothering to show Ellen the way. Ellen made her way down the hall and knocked on the appropriate door.

"Come in." A deep male voice said.

Ellen opened the door and entered the office, which was spacious and well decorated. Wood bookshelves lined three of the walls, their shelves full of leather bound books. The fourth wall was made of glass and overlooked the parking lot.

Eric sat behind a huge wood desk. Everything was meticulously arranged, and Ellen could see a wedding picture of Eric and a much happier version of his wife. Another framed photo of his wife and children was also visible. Eric stood and extended his hand, "What can I do for you?"

He was taller than Ellen remembered. Standing, he was well over six feet. He wore an expensive looking suit, probably Italian. His sandy hair was close cut and his eyes deep set and blue. A five o'clock shadow was noticeable.

"My name is Ellen. I bought your old house on Owl Creek. We met at the closing. I've been trying to reach you. I spoke with your wife…and your friend Josh…from high school." Ellen said.

"My wife told me you stopped by. I don't see how I can help you." He said without expression.

"Look, I don't know how else to say this, so I'm just going to say it." Ellen said, taking a deep breath. "The body of a young woman, Jenny Mathews, was found in the lake behind my house. Also, I found her locket hidden behind a stone in the basement. Do you have any idea how it got there?" She decided to leave out the part about Jenny's unrestful spirit for the time being.

Eric appeared genuinely shocked at the news of Jenny's body being discovered. He quickly regained his composure. "I'm afraid I don't."

"So, you have no idea how her locket came to be hidden in my basement?" Ellen asked.

"No. Why would I?" Eric asked, clearly perturbed.

"Because when she went missing you and your family were living in that house. It stands to reason that one of you hid the locket. Did you know Jenny?" Ellen asked. Though she knew he had been with Jenny the night she disappeared, she wanted to see if he would admit it.

Thankfully, it appeared he decided to go with the truth and said, "I remember Jenny. I didn't know her very well, though. She was only visiting for the summer. A friend of mine lived down the street from her. We all went to the library together…to hang out." He stated.

Ellen couldn't be sure but she suspected he wasn't telling her everything. "Was that the only time you saw her? Did she ever come over to your house?" Ellen asked.

Eric shook his head. "I only met her the one time. That was the night she disappeared. I never saw her again."

"What happened that night?" Ellen asked.

"Nothing really. We met at the corner, walked to the library, hung out for a while, and then went our separate ways. The last time I saw Jenny, she was walking home."

"Alone?" Ellen demanded.

"Look, it wasn't my fault what happened to her. Me and my friend wanted to go to the arcade. Jenny said she had to get home, so we parted ways outside the library. What are you trying to get at anyway?" Eric wanted to know, irritation evident in his voice.

"I'm just trying to find the truth.
That poor girl lost her life and somehow ended
up in a lake owned by you and your family.
Seems coincidental that her body would end up
there *and* you were one of the last people to see
her alive." Ellen concluded.

"I think you should leave. I have
nothing more to say to you." Eric said, standing.

"Very well. You should know, however,
that I've advised the detective working this case
about your connection. He'll be in contact."
Ellen calmly told him. Rising from her chair,
she didn't wait for a response as she walked out
the door.

....

"Do you think he's telling the truth?"
Marcie asked later that evening.

They were sitting at the kitchen table in
Ellen's house, sipping the wine Marcie had
brought with her. Scott was watching tv in the
living room and Natalie was already asleep.

"I don't know. I felt like he was hiding
something…or that he knew more than he was
letting on. But why lie?" Ellen asked, reaching
for her wineglass.

"Maybe he was involved with Jenny's
death. It makes sense, you know? After all,
how else would Jenny's locket end up hidden in

your basement?" Marcie said, her words slightly slurred by the wine. She was on her third glass already.

Ellen got up to pace, wineglass in hand. "I don't know. It just doesn't make sense. Why would Eric kill Jenny? I mean, he barely knew her, right?"

"According to him. Who says he's telling the truth? Maybe they were romantically involved and she gave him the locket. Then, things went south and she broke it off. He may have gotten pissed and offed her." Marcie concluded, gulping down the rest of her wine.

Ellen reached for the bottle and poured the remainder into her friend's glass. "You aren't planning on driving home, are you?"

"Are you insinuating that I am too intoxicated to drive?" Marcie asked, batting her eyelashes innocently.

:We both know you have zero tolerance when it comes to drinking." Ellen said, smiling.

"You're right. Mind if I crash here? I don't want to intrude in case you and Scott have something 'special' planned for later." Marcie said, her mouth curving into a lopsided smile.

"From the sound of things, I don't think Scott is up for anything 'special', as you put it." Ellen told her friend. Scott's snoring could be heard from the living room.

Marcie sighed. "You see what happens? You get married and the romance dies. Sad."

"You're silly!" Ellen exclaimed. "Seriously though. You can stay the night. We'll just leave Scott on the couch and you can sleep with me."

"It'll be like old times! A slumber party!" Marcie said cheerfully.

"Now that that's settled, I just don't know what else I can do about Jenny. This whole thing is crazy. Do you really think Eric and Jenny had a thing?" Ellen asked, regarding her friend, as she began tidying up the kitchen.

"It's totally possible. That kind of thing happens all the time. Don't you ever watch *Forensic Files*?" Marcie asked, getting up and rummaging in the fridge.

"What are you looking for?" Ellen asked.

"Do you have any more wine? Or beer?" Marcie asked.

"Yeah, wino. There's a bottle of Chardonnay on the bottom shelf." Ellen answered, laughing.

"Voila!" Marcie said, as she pulled the bottle out. "Perfect. Let's take this and our glasses up to your room and watch a movie."

"Ok, but you're going to have to explain to Scott in the morning why I'm hung over." Ellen said, gathering the glasses.

….

"Ellen, wake up!" Marcie said.

Ellen came awake slowly, clinging to the fringes of sleep.

Marcie shook her. "Ell, come on. Wake up!"

Ellen opened her eyes. The room was dark, moonlight spilling through the open windows in the bedroom. It took her eyes several seconds to adjust to the dimness. She yawned sleepily.

"Ellen, the most bizarre thing just happened." Marcie was saying.

"Hmmm…what?" Ellen asked, trying to get her bearings.

"I had to pee so I got up and went to the bathroom. I was washing my hands when I looked at the mirror. I saw her. In the mirror." Marcie said.

"Saw who?" Ellen asked, coming fully awake.

"I saw Jenny." Marcie said.

Chapter 23

"Ok, so tell me again what happened." Ellen said.

They were seated cross-legged on the bed, all the lights in the room ablaze. Marcie was clutching a pillow to her chest and she looked genuinely frightened.

"I've never actually seen a real ghost before...just felt them. It was so weird. She was right behind me when I looked in the mirror, but when I turned around...she was gone." Marcie said, her voice agitated.

"Did she say anything?" Ellen wanted to know.

Marcie nodded solemnly. "Yes, Ellen. She said, 'everyone must know the truth'. It was at that point I turned around and she was gone. I was alone in the bathroom."

"Wow. You must've been so scared." Ellen said.

"That's an understatement. That has never happened to me before. What's worse is she looked so...angry. And sad too. What do you think she meant?" Marcie asked.

"I don't know. I guess she wants us to find out what really happened to her. I just wish she would give us a clue or let us know if we're on the right path. I just don't know where to go from here." Ellen said, her voice catching with emotion.

"Me either, but it's obvious she wants us to find out the truth about her murder. We're going to have to really dig deep. I think that we should search the house tomorrow and see if we can uncover anything else that might give us a clue. What do you think?" Marcie asked.

"You're right. As soon as I drop Natalie off, we'll get started. I just hope there's something here." Ellen said with uncertainty.

....

The next morning, the two women were in the attic of Ellen's house. They had spent the better part of an hour tearing apart the basement with no luck of finding anything of value. Now, they stood in the attic, unsure of what to do.

"Maybe there's a loose floorboard." Marcie suggested.

It was a place to start, so both women began prying at the wood floor, hoping one of the planks would give. After nearly fifteen minutes, they came up empty.

"Now what?" Ellen asked.

"Damn! I thought this would be easier. I thought Jenny would lead us in the right direction." Marcie said.

"No such luck. How are you feeling anyway?" Ellen asked.

"What do you mean?" Marcie asked, confused.

"Headache? Nausea? Feeling shaky?" Ellen asked.

"Huh? Oh, no. I feel fine. I think my scare last night eliminated all affects of a hangover. Thanks for asking though." Marcie said, smiling.

"Just checking. I want you in tip top shape for this scavenger hunt." Ellen told her friend.

"Actually, I am thirsty. Do you have any bottled water?" Marcie asked as she felt along the eaves of the attic.

"Sure. I'll get it. I need to use the bathroom anyway." Ellen said.

Making her way to the kitchen, Ellen opened the fridge and confiscated two bottles of water. Before returning to the attic, she made a pit stop at the bathroom. After finishing, she washed her hands and headed down the hall towards the attic entrance.

A sound behind her stopped her in her tracks. Turning around, she tried to find the source of the noise. Nothing. Deciding it was the cat, she continued towards the attic.

Again the sound. A tapping. She listened carefully, holding her breath. After a moment, she exhaled loudly and called out, "Boo?" The cat was nowhere in sight.

Then she heard it again. A loud tapping. It seemed to be coming from Natalie's room. Praying it wasn't another mouse, Ellen entered her daughter's bedroom and paused to listen. Several seconds passed before she heard the tapping again. It appeared to be coming from the closet. Had Boo gotten locked in?

Ellen opened the door and peered inside. No sign of the cat. Ellen poked around for the source of the noise. Perhaps it was one of Natalie's toys. There was no light in the closet and it was too dark to really see, so Ellen went to get a flashlight.

At the foot of the attic, she called up to Marcie, "Hey! Can you come down here? And bring a flashlight with you."

Marcie appeared at the attic entrance, "Why? Did you find something?" she asked, handing Ellen a flashlight.

"I'm not sure. There's a strange tapping noise coming from Natalie's closet. I can't figure out what's causing it?"

"God, I hope it's not another mouse." Marcie said, looking apprehensive.

"I don't think so. I haven't seen a mouse since that time with you. Besides, Boo doesn't seem to enjoy sharing his home with rodents." Ellen remarked, remembering the dismembered carcass of the mouse she had discovered in the kitchen a few weeks ago.

The two women reached the closet and Ellen shone the beam from the flashlight around the interior. Despite belonging to a preschooler, the closet was remarkably tidy and organized. Only one toy was lying on the floor: a stuffed rabbit Ellen had given Natalie for Easter.

"I don't see anything. Are you sure the noise was coming from here?" Marcie asked, tossing the rabbit into the toy bin.

"Hmmm…I thought so. Maybe it was a pipe or something. I did flush the toilet and ran the faucet right before I heard it." Ellen said, turning off the flashlight.

Just as they were turning to leave, a loud banging sound emerged from the closet's interior. The force of the bang was so violent it knocked the lid off of Natalie's toy box.

Marcie jumped, "What the hell was that?"

"I don't know. I'm pretty sure it *wasn't* a pipe though." Ellen said. Despite being frightened, she was curious as to what caused the bang and again turned on the flashlight. The beam shone over the closet's interior: toy bin, a box with some of Natalie's baby clothes, two framed pictures Ellen had yet to hang up. Ellen parted the hangers in the closet, pushing the clothes to either side.

"Whoa, Ell, what's that?" Marcie asked, pointing to the back of the closet.

At first, Ellen wasn't sure what Marcie was talking about, but then she spotted it. The closet was lined in bead board that had been painted a soft yellow. There appeared to be a slight gap between the boards, though. Ellen traced the gap upward with the flashlight. Approximately three feet up, another gap could be detected. It cut across the back of the closet two or so feet and then back down.

"I think it's some kind of door or something." Ellen remarked.

"There's no hinges, though. It must just pull out." Marcie said.

Ellen put down the flashlight and tried to wedge her fingers in the gap. The opening was too small. "See if you can find something to pry it open." Ellen told Marcie.

Moments later, Marcie returned with a putty knife. "Here."

"Where'd you find that?" Ellen asked, taking the putty knife.

"It was on Natalie's dresser." Marcie said.

Puzzled as to why Natalie would have a putty knife in her room, Ellen used the instrument to pry open the door. It took several minutes to break through the paint that sealed the door, but eventually it snapped open. "Grab the flashlight." Ellen said as she leaned the door against the wall outside the closet.

"Is it some kind of secret room?" Marcie asked, shining the flashlight's beam into the opening.

"I don't think so. It's more like a cubby hole." Ellen told her friend, her eyes slowly adjusting to the dimness of the nook.

"There's a box in there. Look." Marcie said.

Ellen reached in and pulled the box out. It was an old packing box, the top covered in dust and cobwebs. Ellen carried the box to the center of the room where the light was better.

"Hurry up and open it." Marcie said, excitedly.

Ellen pried open the flaps and looked inside. "It's a bunch of newspaper articles."

"What do they say?" Marcie demanded impatiently.

Ellen cast a look at her friend.

"Sorry. I'm just excited. Why would someone hide this in that cubby?" Marcie wondered.

"Let's take this down to the kitchen. I'm hungry and thirsty. I'll make us some lunch and we'll go through it all."

....

An hour later, the two women sat at the kitchen table, newspaper articles and the remnants of their lunch littering the tabletop. The house was quiet save for the hum from the refrigerator. The back door was open and a warm breeze blew into the kitchen carrying with it the scent of honeysuckle.

"What does it all mean?" Marcie asked, breaking the silence.

Ellen considered her friend's question. Most of the articles were unrelated; just a collection of different stories ranging from vandalism and theft to missing pets. It seemed there had been a rash of pet-knappings that occurred over a period of six months the same year that Jenny disappeared. Most of the pets had been taken from their yards, never to be seen again. The police had suspected the pets were being sold to either backyard breeders or laboratories. They never had any leads and eventually the thefts stopped.

There were a couple of articles, however, directly related to Jenny's disappearance. They were the same articles that Ellen had read at the library and though they revealed nothing new, it was interesting that someone had saved them.

Equally interesting were the two articles about Josh Masters. At the time, he would've been a teenager. Both articles relayed how he had been caught stealing; once from the local slaughterhouse and another time from a pet store in a nearby town. It seemed that when he was caught at the slaughterhouse, he had in his possession a pig carcass. He had claimed that he did it on a dare. The charges were dropped.

At the pet store, he was caught trying to walk out with a rabbit. This time his defense was that his sister really wanted a rabbit, and he couldn't afford one. The owner of the store, however, was not swayed and Josh was charged with theft.

"I don't know, Marcie. Maybe someone was just collecting articles on crime here in town. Some people do that, God only knows why." Ellen answered her friend as she scanned another article about a vandalized home a few streets over from her own.

"I know people do that, but I don't think that's what this is about. All these articles range over a period of time of about three years starting shortly before Jenny went missing and ending immediately after Emily was killed. Don't you think that's odd?" Marcie wanted to know.

Ellen couldn't deny that it was odd. It would seem that whoever collected the articles was either Emily herself or someone in her family. "Of course it's odd. Do you think it was Emily? And if so, why?"

"I do think it was Emily. As for why, I have no idea. Maybe she was onto something. Maybe she figured out what happened to Jenny by piecing together all these seemingly unrelated crimes." Marcie said.

"That's possible, but it still leaves us in the dark as to who killed them. We don't even know for certain that their deaths resulted by the same person." Ellen said, throwing her arms up in frustration.

"Well, maybe you're unsure, but I am certain that the evidence points directly at Eric." Marcie said matter-of-factly. "First of all, Jenny's body was found on this property-the same property, I might add, that Eric inhabited at the time she died. Next, you discovered a locket belonging to Jenny that someone went to some trouble to conceal. Who else but Eric would have access to the basement? Then, we discover these newspaper articles, also hidden, which strongly suggests that someone-presumably Emily-was suspicious of her brother as well. Next, Emily is killed and Eric does a complete 180, transforming from delinquent to model citizen. And finally, Eric admits to seeing Jenny the night she died. And besides, his wife's a bitch."

"What's that got to do with anything?" Ellen asked.

"Nothing really. I just don't like the woman." Marcie said.

"Everything you say makes sense." Ellen said. "I just wish we could convince Detective Crawley. "

"I think we can now. We need to talk to him together and lay it all out for him. Even a half-rate cop could see the connection." Marcie said, getting up to look in the cabinets.

"What are you looking for?" Ellen asked.

"Got any chocolate? All this detective work makes my blood sugar drop." Marcie said, as she withdrew a package of Oreo's. "These will do nicely."

"Okay. Now that you're no longer in danger of hypoglycemic shock, when should we talk to Detective Crawley?"

"I'm free all day." Marcie said, shoving another Oreo into her mouth.

"Hmmm. I have to pick up Natalie from daycare by six at the latest." She said, glancing at the clock. It was almost 4:00pm.

"Well, we'd better get going." Marcie said, grabbing a handful of cookies for the road.

....

"Okay. I admit there are some bizarre coincidences here, but I'm not convinced that Eric Garritson is a murderer." Detective Crawley said, wiping his brow with a handkerchief and staring pointedly at his watch.

It was quarter till five and Ellen and Marcie were seated in the detective's cramped office. The air conditioning was broke and the temperature in the room was stifling. Marcie was fanning herself with a magazine and Ellen could feel her shirt sticking to the back of the vinyl chair. They had spent over a half-hour explaining their theory to him and neither woman was in the mood for his skepticism.

"What do you mean by coincidences?" Marcie snapped.

"I'm saying I can't arrest a man based on the convoluted story of two housewives with nothing better to do than sit around and play CSI. This isn't a television show, ladies. We need cold hard facts before we can get a warrant to arrest someone." The detective said, clearly annoyed.

"So let me get this straight. Not only are you a moron, but you're also a sexist? For your information, I'm not married and Ellen has a full-time job." Marcie said in reference to the housewife comment.

"There's no reason to call names here. I'm just saying, it's obvious you both have a lot of time on your hands. I mean, you're out interviewing innocent people, accusing them of God only knows what and then you still seem to have time to find hidden passages and dead bodies in the lake!" Detective Crawley said, his face turning red.

"Look," Ellen interjected, "we understand that this whole thing is crazy, but the reality is there *was* a dead body in my lake and there *are* hidden areas in my house. Maybe that's an everyday occurrence for you, but it's a once in a lifetime occurrence for me."

"Don't you find anything we've told you the slightest bit possible?" Marcie demanded.

"I said I'd look into it-and I will. But you've got to give me some time here. I have nothing concrete to go on." The detective explained.

"Nothing concrete?" Marcie asked, incredulous. "What more do you need? You have a dead body, a connection between the deceased and Eric Garritson, and a Goddamned locket of a dead girl hidden in the house he lived in when she died. I mean, seriously, what more evidence do we need to provide you before you admit we're right? Would a signed confession convince you?"

"I have no proof that locket was actually found hidden in the basement. As for Eric's connection to Jenny Matthews? I called him and discussed it with him and his answer seemed very credible to me. During that discussion, he indicated that Mrs. Christiansen here all but accused him of murdering Jenny. You're lucky he's not filing charges against you." Detective Crawley stated.

Ellen couldn't believe her ears. Was this man for real? "File charges against me? I can't believe you. Come on, Marcie. This was a huge waste of time." She said, gathering her purse from the floor.

"Look, I'm sorry you feel that way. I really am. You have to understand my position, though. There are certain ways these things have to be handled." The detective tried to explain.

Ellen barely heard him. She couldn't leave the office fast enough. Back in the car, she sat for a moment willing her anger to subside. She took several long, deep breaths.

"That's bullshit." Marcie was saying.

"Let's forget it for now. I have to pick Natalie up and I don't want her to see me upset." Ellen said, pulling out of the lot.

"Ell, we can't let this go. I know we're right." Marcie said.

"I know we are too. And we're not going to forget it. It's time we take matters into our own hands." Ellen said.

Chapter 24

The next day was Saturday and Scott had convinced Ellen to take Natalie to the county fair. It wasn't that Ellen didn't want to have a little fun and spend time with her family. It was just that she desperately needed to figure out her next move. How was she going to prove that Eric had murdered Jenny and maybe his sister, as well? Perhaps this little reprieve would afford her the opportunity to clear her mind and figure something out.

"Come on, honey! We're ready to go!" Scott was calling to her from downstairs.

Ellen finished brushing her hair and, as an afterthought, threw on a quick coat of mascara and a hint of lip-gloss. Glancing in the mirror, she was pleased with her appearance. The sunny days of summer had given her skin a soft bronze color and though she hadn't noticed before, she had lost a few pounds as well. The shorts she wore were from before she got married and her sleeveless shirt showed off slender, toned arms. Smiling to herself, she ran downstairs.

The drive to the fair was pleasant. They sang along to the radio and talked about their lives. Scott was in an especially good mood as he discussed how he was the only senior salesman chosen to go to an insurance seminar in Las Vegas. "The best part is, I'll have some extra vacation time, so I thought you could go with me and we could spend a little time in the casinos. What do you think?"

"That sounds great. What about Natalie?" Ellen asked.

"She can stay with my parents. I don't think Vegas is the kinda place for a kid." Scott explained.

"But I wanna go!" Natalie protested from the backseat.

Ellen laughed. "We'll talk about it later, sweetie."

Just then, they arrived at the entrance to the fair. Scott pulled up to the booth and paid for parking. He was then directed to park in a field where several cars were already lined up.

As they got out of the car, Natalie asked, "Can we ride the Ferris wheel first?"

"Well, first we have to get tickets." Scott told her, taking her hand.

Together they walked to the main gate and purchased tickets. The attendant explained that the rides weren't included in the general admission price and they would have to buy ride tickets at a separate booth. She also gave them a map of the area, which included the times of different events.

"Wow, I want to check out the rodeo." Ellen said. "It doesn't start till one o'clock though."

"What's a rodeo?" Natalie wanted to know.

While Ellen explained, Scott went in search of the ticket booth for the rides. "Come on, kiddo. Let's get something to drink. I'm thirsty."

"Can I have an ice cream?" Natalie asked.

"Okay." Ellen said and ordered a chocolate kiddie cone for Natalie and a Diet Coke for both herself and Scott. As she finished paying, she spotted Scott.

"Can you believe it? Twenty bucks for ten ride tickets. We'll have to take turns riding with Natalie." He said.

"Yeah? Well, I just dropped $17.50 for two sodas and an ice cream cone." She told him, handing him his drink.

"It seems like when we were kids, the fair was a lot cheaper." He grumbled.

"That's cause we weren't the ones paying for it." Ellen said, taking his hand lightly in hers.

Together, the three of them made their way towards the Ferris wheel. There was already a long line that snaked its way through the crowd. Nearby, a child had dropped his cotton candy and was crying, his mother trying to soothe him. The more she placated him, however, the louder he cried.

"Mommy, will you ride it with me?" Natalie pleaded.

"I don't think so, Natalie. Mommy is afraid of heights. Is it ok if Scott rides the Ferris wheel with you and I ride the bumper cars?" Ellen asked, glancing up at the massive Ferris wheel. She had never liked heights.

"Ok." Natalie said reluctantly. "But you have to also ride the Tilt-O-Whirl with me."

"It's a deal. I'll just wait over there on that bench." Ellen said.

While she waited, Ellen balanced her checkbook. Judging from the long line for the Ferris wheel, it would be a while before Scott and Natalie returned. She might as well make good use of her time.

"Ellen?" A voice interrupted.

Ellen glanced up to see Stan and Noreen Fischer. "Noreen, Stan, how are you?" she said, stuffing her checkbook in her purse and giving both her neighbors a hug.

"We're good, Ellen. How about you? Are you here by yourself?" Noreen asked looking around.

"I'm with my family. They're waiting in line over there." Ellen said, indicating the Ferris wheel.

"Oh, it looks like they'll be a while. We were just about to go have lunch. Did you want to join us?" Noreen asked.

"I don't know. I should probably wait for Scott and Natalie." Ellen explained.

"Dammit, Noreen, leave the woman alone. She probably wants to spend time with her family." Stan said gruffly.

"Oh, it's not that at all. I just don't want Scott wondering where I went off to in case they get out of line before I get back." Ellen said.

"Nonsense. Stan, why don't you go pick us up some lunch and I'll wait here with Ellen. There's a nice picnic bench over there where we can eat." Noreen told her husband.

"Fine. What do you want?" Stan asked.

"A hot dog. Lots of relish and a root beer. Ellen, do you want anything?" Noreen asked.

"No thanks. I'm good." She replied holding up her Diet Coke.

Ellen watched as Stan walked off in search of the nearest hot dog stand. Turning her attention to Noreen, she said, "It's nice to see you again."

"Oh, you too. I was just telling Stan the other day that we should all get together for a barbecue. Wouldn't that be nice?" Noreen asked. "Stan makes the juiciest burgers ever."

"Yes it would be nice. Maybe one night this week? Scott and I usually get home from work by six at the latest." Ellen told the woman.

"Perfect. I'll see what Stan's plans are. It seems like he's been spending more and more time at the golf club. You'd think he'd be improving with all the hours he's been putting in, but I'll tell you the man can't sink a ball to save his life." Noreen said.

Ellen laughed. "Scott likes to golf too. Maybe they can go together sometime."

"That'd be great. I'll mention it to Stan. So, did you ever find out anything about your house?" Noreen asked.

"Um, not really. Just information about the previous owners and stuff like that." Ellen replied.

"I heard about that poor girl they found in your lake. I wanted to come over and check on you but Stan said to leave you alone. He thought you were probably too upset to socialize." Noreen said, raising an over-plucked eyebrow.

"Yes, it was upsetting. I still can't believe it, you know?" Ellen said.

"Who'd of thought? All these years and no one knew where she was. Well, at least her family can give her a proper burial." Noreen said.

"That's true. Did you know that Eric Garritson was one of the last people to see her alive? He was with her the night she disappeared." Ellen stated.

"No, I had no idea. Oh, here comes Stan. Finally." Noreen said.

"I couldn't find any relish, so I got you mustard instead." Stan told his wife, handing over a hot dog.

"That'll do, I suppose. Sit down, Stan. Ellen and I were just talking about that girl they found in her lake." Noreen said.

"Hmph. I remember her. Seemed nice enough." Stan said, wiping mustard from his chin.

"What? You knew her? You never told me that." Noreen said pointedly.

"You knew Jenny?" Ellen asked.

"Yeah. I saw her once. Normally I wouldn't have remembered her at all, but there was an incident." Stan said, glancing at his wife. "I guess it happened shortly before she disappeared. It was late and Gale and Henry were out with friends. They had invited us, but Noreen had a stomach bug, so I stayed home to take care of her. Anyway, she went to bed and I wasn't really tired so I went out for a walk. I passed by the Garritson's and heard voices by the lake. The moon was full and I could see Eric and a girl sitting on that old bench Henry kept under the oak. They were talking and drinking beer."

"What did you do?" Ellen asked.

"I confronted them. They were both standing on the bank, dripping wet and naked. Henry and Gale would've been pissed. Anyway, the girl-Jenny-begged me not to tell. She seemed like a nice enough girl so I never said anything to Gale. Or Henry. Maybe I should've, but it seemed harmless." Stan concluded.

"Stan Fischer, I cannot believe you'd keep something like that from me!" Noreen said, clearly upset.

"Oh, Noreen, it was years ago. Besides, I knew you'd go flapping your jaws to Gale the first chance you got." Stan said.

"Do you think Eric did something to her?" Noreen asked, her eyes widening.

"I don't know. I talked to the detective on the case and he doesn't seem to think so. Still, I'll mention this to him if you don't mind." Ellen said to Stan.

"I don't give a rat's patootie. I'm sure the detective's right, though. Eric may have had his issues, but he didn't strike me as a killer. And they were just kids at the time." Stan said, polishing off the last of his hot dog.

"Mommy, mommy! Did you see me? We were all the way at the top waving." Natalie cried out, running up to Ellen.

"Why, hello, Natalie. Aren't you adorable?" Noreen said to the little girl.

"Hey, Stan, how are you?" Scott asked.

"To be perfectly honest, I'm starting to get a bad case of heartburn." Stan said, rubbing his chest and wincing.

"Probably the hot dog. Or the funnel cake. Maybe it was the burrito." Noreen kidded her husband.

"Who knows? Come on, Noreen. Let's go home. I left my antacids at the house." Stan said, rubbing his stomach.

As they said their good-byes, Ellen promised to call Noreen about getting together for a barbecue. She watched as they walked away.

"Come on, Mommy. Let's go ride another ride!" Natalie squealed.

"Ok, sweetie. Where to?"

The rest of the day passed without incident. Ellen and her family rode rides, ate cotton candy, and watched the rodeo. By the time they arrived home that evening, Ellen was too exhausted to cook dinner, so Scott picked up Chinese food and they picked out a movie on Netflix. They all snuggled on the couch eating Sesame Chicken and fried wontons. By 9:00,

Natalie fell asleep and Scott carried her up to bed.

"Want a glass of wine?" he asked from the living room doorway.

"Sure. Why not?" Ellen answered.

Scott left the room and came back a few minutes later with two glasses of wine. "So, what do you think about Vegas?"

"Sounds too good to be true. A real vacation? That's exactly what I need." Ellen told him, sipping her wine and snuggling up to him, resting her head on his chest.

"Well, then it's set. We'll go. My parents can watch Natalie and you and I can spend a little quality time together. I know things have been hectic since we bought the house. We both could use a little R and R." He said, wrapping his arm around her shoulders.

"Then it's a date." She said, kissing him.

....

The sound of the phone ringing roused Ellen from a deep sleep. Groggily, she reached for her cell phone on the nightstand. "Hello."

"Ell, it's me." Marcie said in a hushed voice.

"Marcie, what time is it?" Ellen asked.

"It's just after midnight. Never mind that. I'm sitting across the street from Eric's

house and guess who just showed up?"
Marcie asked.

"What in the hell are you doing at Eric's
house?" Ellen demanded. "Marcie, get out of
there. You could get hurt."

"They don't know I'm here. Anyway,
Josh just showed up and from the looks of
things they're arguing." Marcie said.

Ellen got out of bed carefully so as not
to wake Scott who had, thus far, been
undisturbed by the phone call. Making her way
down the hall, she crept downstairs to the
kitchen and turned on the light.

"Oh, my God!" Marcie exclaimed.

"What?" Ellen asked her heart in her
throat. Had Marcie been spotted? Was Eric on
his way to her car to confront her?

"Eric's dog just lifted its leg on Josh's
tire." Marcie said.

Ellen breathed a sigh of relief. "Marcie,
you have to get out of there. This is crazy.
Why did you go over there?"

"I was in the neighborhood. Jesse and I
went out for drinks at that new bar that just
opened up on Ridge. Anyway, we left early
cause the place was totally lame. The average
age of the men in the bar was about fifty and-"

Ellen interrupted. "Marcie, I don't care
about that. Why did you go to Eric's house?"

"Well, someone woke up on the wrong side of the bed." Marcie said. "Anyway, I was on my way home and decided to swing by Eric's to see what he was doing."

"What did you expect to see at this hour?" Ellen asked impatiently.

"I don't know…something. And, may I point out, I did see something. No sooner did I park my car and Josh Masters shows up. And I'm telling you, Ell, he looks pissed." Marcie said.

"Are you sure they can't see you?" Ellen asked again.

"I'm not stupid, you know. Trust me, they don't have a clue I'm here. What do you think they're arguing about?" Marcie asked.

"I haven't the foggiest idea." Ellen said.

"Didn't Josh say he hasn't seen Eric recently? Don't you think it's strange that he would show up at his house in the middle of the night?" Marcie wanted to know.

"Yeah, I guess it's strange, but no stranger than you stalking Eric in the middle of the night." Ellen told her friend.

"I'm not stalking him. I was just cruising by. You know, checking things out. If I hadn't come over here-" Marcie cut off her sentence.

"Marcie, what's going on?" Ellen asked.

"Shit. I think they saw me!" Marcie said, and then the phone went dead.

Chapter 25

Ellen sat in the kitchen holding her phone staring at the screen, willing Marcie to call back. When that didn't happen, she dialed Marcie's number, but it went straight to voice mail. What should she do? Call the police? Drive over there herself?

In a fog, she began running around the house, looking for her car keys. She was certain she left them on the hall table, but they weren't there. Then she remembered, they were on the kitchen counter. She had left them there when she had come home from the fair.

Racing into the kitchen, she saw the keys lying on the counter by the back door. She scooped them up and was reaching for her purse on the table when chirping of her phone startled her and she almost dropped it. "Hello." She said, out of breath.

"False alarm." Marcie said.

"Oh, my God, Marcie! Do you have any idea how scared I was? I tried calling back but it just went to voice mail. What the hell happened?" Ellen asked.

"I'm sorry, Ell. I thought they saw me and I got scared and accidentally turned the phone off. I didn't realize it was off until I tried to call you back." Marcie explained.

"What made you think they saw you?" Ellen wanted to know.

"They both looked in my direction, but I guess they must've just heard a noise or something cause neither of them made a move. I took off right after that." Marcie said.

"Where are you now?" Ellen asked with concern.

"Don't worry. I'm on my way home. I'll call you tomorrow, ok? I feel bad for waking you. I guess I was pretty stupid, huh?" Marcie asked, deflated.

"I know you were trying to help and I appreciate that, but Eric may very well have killed two young girls. We have to be careful. From now on, if you get a hair up your ass to go on a stalking spree, call me first and we'll go together. Deal?" Ellen asked.

"Deal. And, Ell?" Marcie said.

"Yeah."

"I love you." Marcie told her with emotion.

Ellen smiled. "I love you too. Now be careful driving home and call me tomorrow. Goodnight."

"Night." Marcie said and hung up the phone.

....

On Sunday morning, Ellen took Natalie with her to the supermarket while Scott went to Home Depot to buy a new grill. They decided to grill barbecued chicken for dinner and Ellen needed to pick up some potato salad and Cole slaw. While passing through the bakery section, she also decided to pick up a pound cake and some fresh strawberries for dessert.

While they were waiting in line to pay, Ellen's attention focused on the cover of one of the local newspapers, *The Daily Examiner*. The headline jumped out at her: *Too Young to Die*. Two side-by-side photos were below the headline: A smiling Emily Garritson on the right and Jenny Matthews on the left.

"How are you today?" the cashier asked Ellen, as she began ringing Ellen's purchases.

Hastily, Ellen handed the girl the paper. "This too, please."

"Oh, I read this article earlier. Hard to imagine, huh? After all these years, they're just now linking these two girls' deaths." The cashier was saying.

Ellen mumbled her agreement and then paid for her groceries. She practically dragged Natalie out the door.

"Mommy, slow down!" Natalie cried out.

"Sorry, baby." Ellen apologized as she forced herself to walk slower.

When they finally reached the car, Ellen took her time strapping Natalie in the backseat. She then carefully placed her packages on the passenger seat and turned the car on. Cranking the AC, she picked up the paper and scanned the article.

Though years have passed since the unfortunate deaths of two teenaged girls, the discovery of one girl's body forces local law enforcement to face the possibility that their deaths were related.

Emily Garritson, age 16, was found strangled to death nearly two decades ago. At the time, police focused their attention on a local man recently released from prison, Morton Stanley. Before police could arrest him, however, Stanley took his own life. Police were compelled to close the case after discovering what they claimed to be undeniable evidence of his guilt.

Just a few years before, however, another girl, Jenny Matthews, went missing after a trip to the library with friends. Jenny was staying with her grandparents for the summer and though an investigation ensued, the case quickly went cold.

A recent turn of events, occurring just weeks ago, has left police baffled. Jenny

Matthews' body was discovered in the lake of a local family. After an autopsy was conducted, it was determined that Jenny had been dead since approximately the time of her disappearance. According to a source, ligatures found on Jenny's body were consistent with those found on Emily Garritson's body. This unexpected twist of events suggests an irrefutable link to the two girls' deaths. Police are refusing to comment at this time.

Ellen felt her blood run cold. How could Detective Crawley keep this information from her? She had point blank asked him if he thought Emily and Jenny's deaths were related and he had been adamant in his denials. Though she knew it was silly, Ellen felt betrayed by the detective's lack of confidence in her. How long had he known? Furthermore, what else was he keeping from her?

....

"Marcie, it's Ellen. Did you read the paper yet?" Ellen asked, as she put groceries away. Marcie mumbled something incoherent and Ellen began to wonder if they had a bad connection. "What?" She asked.

"Sorry, Ell. I was eating Boston cream pie when you called. This shit is the whip.

Have you been to Donnie's bakery recently? Their pies are to die for!" Marcie exclaimed.

"No, I haven't been. Unlike you, if I even look at pie, my ass expands. But nevermind that. Guess what I just read in the paper?" Ellen said and then she read the article to Marcie.

"Whoa! That's heavy stuff. Who do you think the source is?" Marcie wanted to know.

"I don't know, but can you believe that Crawley bastard? I mean, he practically called us meddling nutcases for suggesting Emily and Jenny's cases were connected. I wonder how long he's known about the matching ligatures?" Ellen asked.

"Actually, he *did* call us meddling nutcases. There was no practically to it. As for how long he's known, that's anybody's guess. I seriously doubt he's going to break down and admit anything at this point." Marcie pointed out.

"You're probably right. But why wouldn't he tell us? I mean, the whole town knows now, so what difference would it have made?" Ellen wondered.

"Forget about, him, Ell. We have bigger fish to fry. Who wrote that article? Maybe we can talk to him or her and find out what they know."

"Good thinking, Marcie. Um…let's see." Ellen said as she scanned the article for an author. "Some guy named Nick Russell."

"Ok. I say tomorrow after you get off work, we head straight to his office and find out what he knows. Are you in?" Marcie asked.

"Yeah. Let's meet in the parking lot at the Tan-a-lot. That's sorta halfway between my office and your apartment. Does that work for you?" Ellen asked.

"Actually, that's perfect. I just signed up for a membership there. Figured I'd get a little color before the summer's over." Marcie said.

The two women hung up and Ellen went outside to ask Scott if the grill was ready yet. For some reason, she was famished. She found Scott proudly standing next to the grill. "Is it ready?"

"You bet. Bring the chicken out and I'll whip us up some of the best barbecued chicken this side of the Mississippi." Scott said, a silly grin on his face.

Ellen slapped him on the rear and went inside to get the chicken. As she passed by her cell phone lying on the counter, she noticed the light blinking. She flipped the phone open to see who had called. Private number. As she cleared the call from her screen, she saw that she had a voice mail. As she pressed in her password, she pulled down a plate and got the chicken out of the fridge. And stopped dead in her tracks. The voice on her phone was not one she recognized, but the message was clear: mind your own business or you're next!

….

The next day, Ellen sat in her car at the Tan-a-lot, waiting for Marcie to emerge. She had kept the phone message from Scott, knowing he would just worry, and was dying to share the incident with someone. What was taking her so long?

While she waited, Ellen looked over some files she had brought home from work. Try as hard as she could, she had found it difficult to concentrate on work and now she was behind. She had to get these files completed before tomorrow.

Just as she was becoming engrossed in one of the files, busily jotting notes in the margin, the passenger door swung open and Marcie climbed inside. "Wow. I think I'm burned. Can you crank the AC, please?" Marcie asked, fanning herself with a file folder.

Ellen obliged and glanced at her friend. Sure enough, Marcie's face, neck and shoulders were a dark shade of pink. "How long did you stay in?"

"Too long, obviously. The girl that works there told me I'd be fine for the whole time, which was 20 minutes. I think my skin started smoldering after ten minutes."

"Hmmm. Well, at least next time, you'll know better. Now, I want you to hear something." Ellen told her as she dialed her voice mail and keyed in the password. Then she handed the phone to her friend.

"Shit. Who the hell left that?" Marcie asked.

"I don't know. I think whoever it was tried to disguise their voice, but I'm pretty sure it's a man. What do you think?"

"I'll bet it was Eric. He's the only one who would have a reason to leave a threatening message like that." Marcie said.

"I don't know. Whoever it was, though, seriously freaked me out. I barely got any sleep last night and I was completely unproductive at work today. I don't know how much longer I can put up with this." Ellen said, exasperated.

"Don't worry, Ell. We're going to get to the bottom of this. Come on. Let's go see that reporter fellow and find out what he has to say. Who knows? Maybe he'll even be hot." Marcie said.

Rolling her eyes, Ellen put the car in drive and made her way across town to Edgewood where the office of the Post was located. The newspaper was in a two story brick building situated between a pizza parlor on the left and a funeral home on the right. Ellen parked the car in a visitor's spot and the two women made their way inside.

The lobby was bleak and unadorned, save for a few potted palms and a security desk in the center of the room. Ellen approached the guard behind the desk. "Hi. My name is Ellen and this is Marcie. We're here to see Nick Russell."

"Uh-huh. Do you have an appointment?" The tired looking guard asked.

"Um, actually no, but-"

Marcie cut her off. "We're here to discuss the story he ran in the paper yesterday. About the two girls that died. We have information we think he'd want to hear."

"Oh, yeah? You and a few hundred other loonies." The guard said

Marcie gasped. "Listen here, mister!"

"Darren." The guard interrupted.

Ellen shushed Marcie and tried again. "Ok, Darren. My name is Ellen Christiansen. They found that girl's body in *my* lake. We recently uncovered some interesting information that the police don't seem to want to hear, most likely due to their obvious incompetence. We thought that perhaps Mr. Russell would find the information newsworthy, but if you think we're a couple of loonies, that's fine. We'll take our story elsewhere." She finished and then turned to walk away.

"Hold on a minute." The guard said, and he picked up the phone and spoke quietly into the receiver.

Marcie nudged Ellen and winked at her. Ellen smiled, but held her breath, praying Nick Russell would agree to see them.

"Ok. Mr. Russell will be right out. You can just wait here." The guard said, as he sat back down and began reading a *Fisherman's Weekly.*

A few minutes later, a man, probably in his mid thirties, walked into the lobby. He was tall and well built, wearing jeans and a black crewneck T-shirt that showed off some very obvious muscle definition. His hair was thick and sandy colored and curled slightly in the back. Ellen glanced at Marcie who was practically drooling. It seemed she had gotten her wish. Nick Russell was indeed hot.

As he approached them, he extended a hand. "Hi. I'm Nick Russell. You must be Ellen."

"Yes, and this is my friend Marcie." Ellen told him as they shook hands.

"Hello." Marcie said, extending her hand. "I don't think I've ever met a real reporter before."

"Well, we're just ordinary people, I assure you." He said, his smile broadening as he took Marcie's hand and kissed it.

Marcie giggled and tossed her hair back over her shoulder. "Well, aren't you charming?"

Ellen cleared her throat and suggested that maybe they could go to Nick's office to talk.

"Actually, I don't have my own office. Just a cubicle. But maybe we could talk in the conference room." He told them as he led the way down a hallway and into a large room filled with tiny cubicles and people bustling around. At the far end of the room, they entered another, much smaller, room that held a large executive table with several black, leather chairs. He held one chair out and indicated to Marcie that she should have a seat. Ellen pulled her own chair out and sat down.

"So," Ellen began. "I read your article in the paper yesterday. I guess you already know that it was my lake that Jenny Matthew's' body was found in. I'm just interested to know how you found out about the autopsy results? Detective Crawley told me there was nothing informative about the results when I asked."

A wide grin spread across Nick's face and he wagged a finger at her. "Uh-uh. You know I can't reveal my source."

"Ok. Fine. It's just…" Ellen looked to Marcie for assurance. Marcie nodded, so Ellen continued. "Look, some strange things have happened to me and my family since we moved in that house. And Detective Crawley won't take any of it seriously."

"What kind of 'things' are you talking about?" Nick asked, clearly intrigued.

Again, Ellen looked at Marcie for support. The other woman said, "It's ok, Ell. Tell him everything." And she did. She told him every detail of the last few months starting with the day they moved in and ending with the threatening message from the night before.

For a while, no one spoke. They all just kinda sat there mulling over what was said, each lost in their own thoughts. The only sound was that of an airplane flying somewhere off in the distance. Ellen began to have doubts about telling Nick. What if he freaked out and told them to leave?

Finally, Nick cleared his throat and spoke. "Wow. That's a very interesting story. I must say, it's been a while since I've heard anything so…bizarre."

"So you think we're making it up, huh?" Ellen asked softly.

"No. Not at all. I just can't believe that, after what you've told me, no one else believes you. I mean, it all makes sense in a sorta irrational way." Nick said, a corner of his mouth turning up in a half smile. "But I *do* believe you. Do you think I could come over sometime? To your house, I mean."

"Um, sure, but why?" Ellen asked.

"I want to see if I can...feel anything. I've never seen a ghost before. I think it would be interesting." He said.

"You're not going to print any of this are you?" Marcie demanded.

Ellen hadn't even thought of that possibility. The mere thought made her stomach clench. They would be the laughing stock of the neighborhood.

"No. Of course not. At least, not right now. And never if you don't want me to. But I really think this story is something other people would appreciate. I mean, surely there are other people out there that have had this kind of experience and felt alone and isolated like you have." Nick said with conviction.

"I don't' know." Ellen said, hesitantly. "I can't even think about that right now. I just need some help putting an end to this whole thing. The truth is, I just don't know where to go from here. Jenny's ghost wants me to do something and I'm not sure what. All I know for sure is that I need to do *something*. And soon."

"Ok. Fair enough. How about I stop by your house tomorrow evening? Around 6:00?" he asked.

Ellen agreed and then stood to leave. "Thanks for listening and not thinking I'm crazy. You have no idea what that means."

"No problem. Thanks for sharing your story. You're a brave woman." Nick said.

Back in the car, Marcie said. "Holy shit! That man is beautiful!"

Ellen laughed. "I must admit, he's easy on the eyes. More importantly, though, he believed us."

"I think I'm in love." Marcie said dreamily.

"I'm pretty sure the feeling is mutual. So, can I assume you'll also be coming over tomorrow?"

"Are you kidding? I wouldn't miss it for the world. And not just because Nick's so adorable. You know I want to help put an end to this." Marcie said with emotion.

"I know, silly. I'm just giving you a hard time. The question is, how am I going to tell Scott? I mean, I've practically kept him in the dark about everything that's been happening." Ellen said.

"I'll try to think of something. In the meantime, can we please stop and get something to eat? I'm starving!" Marcie said.

Chapter 26

On Tuesday, Ellen arrived early at work to get a jump on the day. Andrew was due in court at 11:00 and needed some background work completed, so Ellen pushed herself as hard as she could. As he was preparing to leave, she handed him the files.

"Hey, thanks, Ellen. I was worried you wouldn't get these done in time." He said.

"Listen, about that. I'm really sorry I've been kinda out of it lately. I've just had some crazy stuff going on at home. I promise it's almost over, though. Just please don't fire me." Ellen said.

Her boss laughed. "Not to worry. Even if your head has been in the clouds, you've still managed to get everything done on time. And your work is always flawless. I was starting to worry you were going to quit."

"Are you kidding? You're the best boss ever. I could never quit. I love my job."

"Glad to hear it. I've gotta run. If you need any time off, just let me know. Though it'll be rough, we'll manage without you. I just want you to work through whatever's bothering you." He said sincerely.

"Thanks, Andrew. I really appreciate that, but I'm okay right now. Good luck in court!" Ellen told him and watched as he walked out the door.

Back at her desk, Ellen called Marcie. "Is everything a go for this evening?" she asked her friend.

"Yeah, and I've come up with a plan to get Scott out of the house for a couple of hours. My cousin wants some insurance advice. I thought Scott would be perfect for the job. You think he'll go for it?" Marcie asked.

"I'll give him a call, but if I know Scott, he'll definitely be up for it. He *loves* insurance. Weird, I know, but he's good at it." Ellen told her friend with a laugh.

After hanging up with Marcie, Ellen called Scott and asked him if he could meet with Marcie's cousin. He happily agreed and Ellen gave him directions to Jesse's apartment.

"Do you want me to make dinner?" She asked.

"No. I'll just pick something up on my way. What are you and Natalie going to eat?" He wanted to know.

"Probably leftovers. There's still a ton of barbecued chicken left. I'll heat that up and maybe make some macaroni and cheese. You know how much Natalie likes it." Ellen told her husband.

"Alright then. I have to get to a meeting. I'll see you later. Love ya." Scott said.

"I love you too." She said and hung up. Guilt washed over her. Damn. She hated deceiving her husband. She could only hope that he would forgive her in the end.

....

On her way home from work, Ellen stopped at the supermarket and picked up two bottles of Pinot Grigio. She didn't know if the occasion really called for wine, but it was best to be prepared. As an afterthought, she also picked up some meats and cheeses in case anyone was hungry. She figured she could throw together a charcuterie board to go with the wine.

Once she left the market, Ellen dropped by Natalie's daycare center and picked up her daughter. Natalie was in an especially good mood after finding out she was awarded student of the month. Ellen expressed how proud she was and stopped and got Natalie an ice cream sundae from *Creamy Delights.*

When Ellen finally pulled in her driveway, she saw that Marcie was already there. Her jeep was parked in the driveway and Marcie was perched in one of the white rockers on the front porch. As Ellen and Natalie exited the car, Marcie stood up and waved.

"Aunt Marcie! What are you doing here?" Natalie squealed.

"I just stopped by to see your mom." Marcie explained, scooping the little girl up in her arms. "A special friend of mine is coming over that I wanted you guys to meet."

"Cool!" Natalie said.

"Come on, Nat. Let's go inside and I'll make you something to eat." Ellen said.

"Ok. Can I have some of that cheese you bought?" Natalie asked.

Marcie shot Ellen a questioning look.

"I picked up some meat and cheeses in case anyone was hungry. I figured it was quick and simple." Ellen explained.

While Marcie colored with Natalie at the dining room table, Ellen put the charcuterie board on the table and chilled the wine. Pouring herself a glass, she called out to Marcie and asked if she wanted any. Marcie agreed, so Ellen poured a second glass. Making two trips, she carried everything into the dining room.

"Look at my picture, mommy." Natalie said, showing Ellen a brightly colored picture in her Little Mermaid coloring book.

"That's good, sweetheart." Ellen told her. "Do you really want some of this or should I make something else?"

"I want to try it." Natalie said emphatically.

Ellen dished a couple of slices of pastrami onto a plate and sat it in front of her daughter.

"Mmmm. This is good." Natalie said, her mouth full.

"This is good." Marcie said, shoving a sliver of prosciutto into her mouth.

"Well, I'm glad everyone likes it." Ellen said, helping herself to some of the creamy Brillat Savarin cheese.

Just then, the doorbell rang. Ellen jumped up and went to answer it. Nick stood at the door, dressed in khaki shorts and a pale blue polo shirt. He had a bouquet of fresh cut flowers in one hand and a bottle of red wine in the other. He handed both to Ellen as she stood back and beckoned for him to come in.

"These are lovely. Thank you. Let me show you to the dining room. Oh, and my daughter's here. I really haven't told my husband everything that's going on. He's kinda...grounded. I told Natalie that you were Marcie's friend. Okay?" Ellen said as she led Nick to the dining room.

"No problem." Nick said.

As soon as they entered the dining room, Marcie sprang to her feet. "Hi, Nick. How are you?

From the look on Nick's face, he was more than happy to see Marcie. "Hi, Marcie. Good to see you again."

"Natalie, are you almost finished eating? I thought maybe you could go watch a couple of episodes of Spongebob before bedtime." Ellen said as she arranged the flowers in a vase and sat them in the center of the dining table.

"Ok, mommy." Natalie said as she got up from the table and went into the living room and turned on the tv.

Turning to Nick, Ellen asked, "Would you like something to eat?"

"Sure. Thanks." Nick said, taking a piece of Gouda and some Genoa Salami and popping it into his mouth.

"So, where do you want to start?" Ellen asked.

"Um, I don't know. How about the basement? That's where most of the strange things happened, right?" Nick asked, picking up another piece of sushi.

"At first, but we've experienced incidents in most of the house at this point." Ellen told him.

"Well, the basement is as good a place as any to start, right?" Nick said.

With Ellen leading the way, the trio made their way into the basement. Ellen leaned against the washer and said, "This is it. Over there is the old coal room where I found the locket and I was standing right here when I felt someone breathing on my neck."

Nick took his time poking around behind the furnace and running his hands along the concrete blocks in the coal room. He remained silent for the most part and finally threw his hands up. "I guess she doesn't want to talk to me."

"I wouldn't take that as a bad thing." Marcie said.

"Do you want to walk through the rest of the house?" Ellen asked.

Nick agreed and she gave him a tour of the remainder of the house. Once that was concluded, Ellen showed him the box with all the newspaper clippings in them. He glanced at most of them, but read a few more thoroughly. When he was finished, he looked up. "Did you notice anything about these articles?"

"Like what?" Marcie asked, getting up to refill her wineglass.

"Look." He said, spreading several articles out on the kitchen table. "They're almost all written by Abigail Freeman. Even the ones that weren't written exclusively by her mention her somewhere in the article."

"Huh. I hadn't noticed that before." Ellen said. "Do you know her?"

"Not personally, but I've heard of her. She wrote for the *Crescentville Chronicle* for several years before she broke the story on Emily's death. That story catapulted her career. Now she's the editor in chief of the *Chronicle*."

Ellen considered this information. "That's interesting. So, do you think these articles were saved because Abigail wrote them?"

Nick shrugged. "I don't know really. I just think it's strange that someone took the time to save all these random articles that coincidentally all seem to have been written by the same woman."

"So, where do we go from here?" Marcie asked.

"If you don't mind, I'd like to take these articles with me to the office." Nick said. "Maybe I can do some research and find a connection we're overlooking."

Ellen nodded. "Sure. Take them. But do you really think the answer lies in these articles?"

"What else do we have to go on?" Nick asked.

"Nick," Ellen began. "I know you can't reveal your source, but can you at least tell me if there's a link between your source and anything that I've told you."

"To be honest with you, I don't know who gave me the information on Jenny's autopsy." Nick said. "I came into work one day and there was a package left for me. No return address, but it contained a copy of the autopsy results, police reports, and there was a handwritten note telling me there was a connection between Jenny's death and Emily Garritson's murder."

"The only connection is Eric Garritson." Marcie said. "I mean, he knew Jenny Matthews well enough to have her over to his house *and* he was Emily's brother. What more evidence do we need?"

"Unfortunately, the police are going to need more to go on. But I agree, Marcie. There is definitely a connection between Eric in both Jenny and Emily's deaths. We just have to figure it out." Nick said.

"I just don't know what else to do." Ellen said, clearly exasperated. "I mean, I've pretty much talked to everyone I can think of that might know something."

Marcie jumped up and began pacing. "What if you interviewed Eric, Nick? I mean, you just ran that story. It wouldn't be suspicious if you wanted to do a follow up with one of the victim's brothers. What do you think?"

"I don't know." Nick said, running his fingers through his hair. "I guess I could try, but from what you tell me, Eric doesn't wanna talk."

"That's true, but it's worth a shot, right?" Marcie asked.

"I'll see what I can do. In the meantime, I'm going to get back to the office and see what I can come up with after going through these articles. I'll call you in a day or two and let you know what I find out." He said, standing.

Marcie practically knocked the table over in her frantic attempt to bid farewell to Nick. "I'll see you to the door." She said, smiling demurely and taking his arm and leading him down the hallway.

"Goodbye, Nick." Ellen called out, though she doubted he heard her, his attention focused on Marcie.

She took the opportunity to check on Natalie, who was snuggled on the couch, her gaze transfixed on the TV. Ellen asked the little girl if she needed anything and Natalie shook her head, then changed her mind and asked for a glass of milk. Ellen fetched the milk, sat it on the coffee table, and then went back to the kitchen.

Marcie returned a few minutes later, her face beaming. "He asked me if I was free for dinner sometime. I didn't want to seem too desperate, so I told him we might be able to get together Thursday or Friday. Do you think I should've held out for Saturday?"

"I wouldn't put him off for too long, Marcie. A man that good-looking probably has women throwing themselves at him." Ellen said, picking up Nick's wineglass and taking it to the sink to wash.

Just then, the backdoor opened and Scott came trudging in, carrying his briefcase and a McDonald's bag. "Who was that pulling out of the driveway just now?" he asked.

"That," Marcie said, "may very well be my future husband."

"Huh. I don't even want to know. Just invite me to the wedding. Did you guys eat dinner? I stopped on my way home and picked up a hamburger. I guess I should've called to see if you wanted anything."

Ellen dried off her hands and went over to kiss her husband. "We're fine, honey. I picked up some meats and cheeses and we munched on that. Natalie even ate some, if you can believe that. You know what a picky eater she is"

"Where is the little tyke?" Scott asked, pulling his burger out of the greasy bag and unwrapping it.

"Watching television. I just took her some milk." Ellen told her husband, handing him a napkin.

"So, how did things go with Jesse?" Marcie asked.

"Good. She really seems to know what she's doing. I went over a few insurance options with her and she's going to look them over and let me know later this week." Scott answered.

"I really appreciate your helping her, Scott. It means a lot." Marcie said sincerely.

"What are friends for?" Scott said.

"Anyway, I should get going and let you guys do the whole family thing." Marcie said, gathering her things.

Ellen walked her to the door and they agreed to talk again over lunch Thursday.

....

Later that evening, after Natalie was in bed, Boo curled up next to her, Ellen and Scott sat in the living room watching TV. Ellen was having trouble concentrating on the program, a reality show Scott had been dying to see.

"You ok?" Scott asked.

"Huh? Yeah, I just can't really get into this." Ellen said, nodding towards the TV.

"Wanna watch something else?" He asked.

"No, sweetie. I know you've really wanted to see this. I think I'm just going to go to bed and read. There are some files I need to go over for work." Ellen told him, standing up. She bent over and gave him a kiss and then headed upstairs.

After changing into an oversized T-shirt, she pulled down the covers and crawled into bed. Taking out one of five files she had brought home from work, she began scanning the contents. She focused her attention on the words before her, and after a while she found herself completely absorbed in her work. As she stared down at the file, she began to feel a little woozy and she watched as a single drop of blood fell onto the top page of her file. She felt a warm stream of blood on her face, running from her nose down her lips and chin.

"Shit." She softly swore then jumped up, tossing the covers aside and making a mad dash for the doorway. Padding down the hall, she tried to remember the last time she had had a nosebleed. Years, she decided absently, as she scrambled into the bathroom and snatched up a wad of tissues from the dispenser that sat atop the toilet. The blood was flowing fast now; the front of her T-shirt stained a dark crimson. She recalled from earlier nosebleeds that she should

tilt her head back to stop the bleeding. She
sat on the toilet, her head back and waited for
the bleeding to stop.

Several minutes passed, and she thought
the flow of blood had eased. She decided to
chance looking in the mirror. Keeping her head
back, she rose from the toilet seat and edged
over to the mirror. As her eyes focused on her
reflection, she was momentarily confused as the
image in the mirror wavered and changed shape.
The reflection before her was that of Jenny
Matthews. Ellen felt the room begin to spin and
her vision began to lose focus. She frantically
grabbed for the sink, but everything suddenly
went black and Ellen lost all sense of the present
time.

*It was so dark. She tried to remember
where she was, but her memory wouldn't
comply. The last thing she did remember was
leaving the library, her arms weighted down
with several books for her summer reading
assignment. She had said good-bye to her
newfound friends and then walked off in the
direction of her grandparent's house.*

*So where was she now? And why
couldn't she remember how she got here?*

*Her head throbbed and she reached up
with her right hand and gingerly probed her
scalp. Her fingers swept across something thick
and sticky and her hair felt matted. There was a*

deep gash at the back of her head.
Frightened, she pulled her hand away quickly.

Panic began to take hold and she tried to stand up. She managed to lift herself up into a squatting position before the pain in her head sent waves of nausea coursing through her body. She doubled over and wretched, her hands clutching her stomach. She forced herself to calm down and take slow, deep breaths.

After a while, the nausea subsided and the pain in her head lessened enough for her to try to stand again. Though shaky, she managed to get all the way on her feet. She tried to focus on her surroundings. It was so dark, though. And cold.

It was then she heard a nearby door opening. Someone was coming.

Ellen gasped out loud and then stumbled backwards towards the bathtub. Arms flailing, she tried to grab something to keep from falling, but all she could grasp was the shower curtain. It ripped away from the rod, her weight pulling it down, and she toppled backwards, landing in a heap at the bottom of the bathtub, the shower curtain tangled all around her.

Scott must've heard the commotion because he came running into the bathroom at that moment. "Ellen, are you ok? What happened?"

"I'm ok." She muttered, trying to dislodge herself from the shower curtain.

"Oh, my God! You're bleeding, honey!" He cried out, noticing the blood on her shirt.

She tried to calm him down. "It's okay, Scott. It was just a nosebleed. I must've gotten dizzy and fallen."

He took her by the arm and led her into the bedroom and gently eased her down onto the bed. "Let me get you a clean shirt."

She watched as he rummaged through the dresser drawers, anxiously searching for a shirt. He snatched up a gray button down flannel and rushed back to her side. "Here, lift your arms." He told her as he pulled off the bloodstained T-shirt and replaced it with the clean flannel.

He then dashed off to the bathroom, only to return moments later with a wet wash cloth. "You've got blood all over your face." He explained as he gingerly dabbed her face with the cloth.

She passively sat there and allowed him to clean her up. She felt detached from the whole scenario. Maybe she was in shock, she thought. She vividly recalled the dream-or whatever it was-and tried to make sense of it, but her mind simply wouldn't focus. The weight of everything she'd been through came crashing down on her, leaving her feeling crushed and full of despair. She began to sob uncontrollably.

Scott pulled her to him and gently stroked her hair. "Shh, honey. It's ok. Everything's ok now."

She wasn't sure how long she cried, Scott holding her and whispering reassuring things. She simply let the emotions that had been building finally bubble over. Before long, she began to babble, at first incoherently, but then with clarity and conviction. She told Scott everything. She expressed her feelings, her utter terror at what had been happening to her. She told him of all the lies. She explained how difficult this had all been on her; how she had felt alone, save for Marcie. She told him that she needed him to understand, to fully believe her. She explained how rotten she felt for keeping him in the dark about so much. Throughout it all, he listened and held her. He kissed her gently and told her he loved her. Eventually, the comfort he offered, along with her utter exhaustion, allowed her to fall asleep.

Chapter 27

Ellen awoke the next morning, on Wednesday, to Scott softly calling her name. "What time is it?" she asked sleepily.

"Almost 9:00am." Scott told her as he kissed her on her forehead.

The night before came crashing back to her in vivid clarity. "Damn. I need to get ready for work. I'm late."

"Don't worry about that. I called Andrew-don't be mad. I told him we had a family emergency and you couldn't come to work. He said not to worry. I also took the day off." He explained.

"Scott, I can't stay home. I have so much work to do. Andrew needs the McKinney file for court today." Ellen said, flinging the covers aside.

Scott gently pushed his wife down. "Don't worry about it. Andrew stopped by this morning and I gave him the file."

"Why?" Ellen asked, confused.

"Sweetie, you have to rest. Whatever is happening to you is taking its toll. And besides, we need to talk. I haven't been here for you like I should've been. That changes starting right now. We're going to work through this. I love you and whatever it is you've been going through, I want to understand." Scott said.

Ellen took a moment to ponder her husband's heartfelt words. "Do you mean it? Do you believe me?"

Scott nodded emphatically. "Absolutely. I don't understand it all, but I believe you, sweetheart. After last night, the sheer terror I saw on your face, I believe you. We're going to get through this. I haven't the foggiest idea how, but I promise you don't have to face this alone. Ok?"

"Oh, Scott." Ellen said, running her fingers through his hair. "I knew there was a reason I married you."

Chuckling, he replied, "And here I thought you married me for my superior wit and all too astonishing good looks."

"That too." Ellen said, laughing.

Just then, Natalie walked in. "Can we have pancakes for breakfast?"

Ellen looked at Scott and both of them burst into laughter.

"What's so funny?" the little girl asked.

"Ok. So, we know that Eric Garritson was with Jenny the night she disappeared?" Scott asked as he absently chewed on a piece of toast.

"Yeah, and that's all we know. For sure." Ellen said, reaching for another slice of bacon.

It was just before 10:00 am and Ellen was seated at the kitchen table with her husband and daughter. They were going over everything that had happened over the past few months, Ellen trying to fill her husband in on the details.

"Who's Eric?" Natalie asked, her mouth full of French toast, powdered sugar smeared all over her chin.

Scott patiently explained. "Eric is the man we bought our house from, kiddo."

"Oh. Can I go watch TV?" Natalie asked, clearly bored with the conversation.

Scott and Ellen exchanged glances. Though they tried to limit Natalie's exposure to television, they couldn't expect a child to understand the current situation at hand. Scott spoke up first, "Um, sure, Natalie. Today is a special day. You can go watch TV if you want.

"Thanks!" She squealed, pushing her chair back and running off to the living room, Boo close on her heals.

"Wow. I wish I could be that excited about television." Scott said, snatching up the last piece of bacon.

Ellen chuckled. "Can you blame her? This conversation is going nowhere, and fast."

Scott looked at his wife. "Look, I know we're repeating the same stuff, but you have to remember that I'm a newcomer to the situation."

Ellen reached across the table and took her husband's hand. "I'm sorry, honey. I didn't mean to make you feel bad. It's just; I don't know how Eric ties into this. Marcie is convinced he's involved, but I don't know."

"Ok. I hear what you're saying. So, you don't think Eric killed Jenny?" he asked.

"I don't know, Scott. I really don't. Detective Crawley doesn't see a connection, but I don't know how seriously he's taking the case. I mean, in his defense, it's been over 20 years." Ellen said.

"Whoa! So, you're defending him now?" Scott asked.

"No. Not defending him. Just playing devil's advocate. You know I think he's a complete asshole." Ellen stated.

Scott reached across the table and took his wife's hand, "I know, sweetie. I just don't get it, you know? If it was Eric, what's the motive?"

Ellen let out a frustrated sigh and ran her fingers through her tangled hair. "That's just the thing, Scott. I don't have the answers. I haven't the foggiest notion why *anyone* would kill another person, let alone why Eric would kill Jenny. I mean, they were both so young. What could she have done to warrant being murdered?"

"Maybe it wasn't murder." Scott said, "Maybe it was an accident."

Ellen considered this possibility. Admittedly, she hadn't really thought too much about the idea that Jenny's death had been an accident. Still, it didn't make sense. She'd had that strange dreamlike vision of Jenny being held captive. Not to mention the autopsy report suggested strongly that she had been bound. How could that have been an accident?

Scott was staring at his wife expectantly. "So, why are you so convinced it was murder?" he asked.

She tried to explain the vision, the dream of Jenny in the lake, the autopsy report, and her own nagging gut feeling that Jenny's death was murder. Scott listened closely, nodding occasionally. When she was finished, she asked, "So, based on all that information, do you still think it could've been an accident?"

"I guess not. It's just all so crazy, you know? I mean, why the hell is all this happening now? Why not 20 years ago when it all actually took place?" Scott wanted to know.

"Your guess is as good as mine, though Noreen Fischer did say that Gail Garittson did complain of strange things happening to her. Maybe Gail just wasn't as open to…spiritual intervention." Ellen said.

Scott chuckled. "Spiritual intervention, huh?"

"You know what I mean. What would you call it, smarty pants?" Ellen joked.

Getting up from the table to clear the dirty dishes, Scott said, "I guess that's as good of a description as any. So, what's our next move? We've got all day to figure something out."

"I don't know. Maybe hit the library again?" Ellen suggested.

"Well, first things first. Could you please go brush your hair? It's sticking up all over the place and looks like a wild animal took refuge in it. I can't be seen in public with you looking like that." Scott said, grinning widely at his joke.

Ellen threw a dishtowel at him and said, "Hey, I'm not the only one that could use some attention in the hygiene department. Have you showered at all this week?"

"Oh, yeah? Well, last one to the shower's a rotten egg!" he called out as he scrambled from the kitchen and dashed for the bathroom.

Laughing, Ellen jumped up and chased him down the hall.

....

"Why do I have to go to Grandma's?" Natalie whined from the backseat. It was just after 11:00am and Ellen and Scott had decided they could accomplish more if Natalie was stowed away somewhere safe.

Ellen turned around in her seat and looked at her daughter. "Because, sweetheart, Daddy and I have boring errands to run and we thought you would have more fun at Grandma's house. She said she might even take you to the zoo."

"Really?" Natalie asked, her face brightening at the thought.

"Sure thing, kiddo!" Scott added excitedly.

Natalie busied herself in the backseat coloring in her *Dora the Explorer* coloring book, seemingly content about a visit with her grandparents. The drive didn't take too long and before she knew it, Ellen was waving goodbye to her daughter who stood on the front porch of her grandparent's house, her grandmother standing next to her.

Just as they were pulling out of the driveway, Ellen's phone rang. Rummaging through her purse, she extracted her phone. "Hello."

"Ellen? Hey, it's Nick. I just got off the phone with Abigail Freeman and she's agreed to meet with us today. I know it's late notice, but I went ahead and made an appointment for 1:00pm. Is that ok?"

"Uh, sure. I'm surprised she could fit us in this quickly." Ellen said.

"Yeah, well, I might've misled her a little as to the reason for the meeting. Just a little white lie, you know. Even with my cover story, I didn't think she'd agree to meet so soon." Nick explained.

"What'd you tell her?" Ellen wanted to know.

"I told her that you had received some new evidence to suggest that Emily Garritson was killed by someone other than Morton Sullivan and that you had approached me about it. I also told her that I no longer wanted to work for the *Examiner* and that if she would entertain the idea of hiring me, I'd let her paper leak the new story." Nick said. "You wouldn't believe how excited she got. Took the bait hook, line, and sinker."

"Wow, Nick. That's pretty creative. What are we going to tell her once we get there?" Ellen asked.

"Don't worry about it. I'll do all the talking. Let's meet at the *Chronicle* a little before 1:00pm and we'll go over some of the details, ok?"

Ellen agreed and hung up the phone. She quickly filled Scott in on the situation. He seemed excited to be involved and suggested they spend the time they had left, before they had to meet Nick, scouring the Internet for any potential leads.

....

An hour and forty minutes later, Ellen and Scott sat waiting in their car in the parking lot of the *Chronicle*. The wind outside was picking up and the local weatherman predicted a nasty storm by late afternoon.

"So, let me get this straight." Scott said from the driver's seat. "All those articles you found were supposedly written by Abigail Freeman?"

"Well, they *all* weren't written by her, but she was at least mentioned in the ones that weren't. It just seems a bit odd." Ellen remarked as she strained her neck, trying to spot Nick's car.

"Hmmm. And you say you found them in Natalie's room?" He asked.

"Yeah. In her closet hidden behind a secret panel. I think that room must've been

Emily's and she's the one that hid them there." Ellen said.

"But why?" Scott asked. "I mean, what could it all mean?"

Ellen took her husband's hand and kissed the knuckles softly. "I'm not sure, honey. That's what we're doing here. Hopefully, Nick can elicit the answers we need from Abigail."

Just then, Nick's car turned into the parking lot and headed down the aisle towards them. He pulled in adjacent to them and parked. Waving, he hopped out of his car and walked over to the rear passenger door of Ellen's car and jumped in.

"Wow, the wind is really picking up out there." He remarked as he slid into the backseat. "So, here's the game plan. I'm gonna do most of the talking, if that's ok. Hopefully, Ms. Freeman won't get too upset once she finds out the real reason we're here."

The three of them quickly gathered their things and exited the car. The wind had really picked up and the skies were dark overhead, the threat of rain eminent. Together, they raced to the front door, pulling it open just as the skies opened up and a torrential rain came pouring down.

Once inside, Nick quickly made his way to the front desk and announced their arrival.

While he chatted up the security guard, Ellen took a look around. The lobby was massive, with huge marble pillars that reached all the way up to the second floor. White granite tiles covered the floors and large, potted exotic plants and flowers added a splash of color. Adorning the richly colored walls were oil paintings of various tropical scenes.

Coming up behind her, Scott remarked, "Geez, business must be booming. This place is nice."

Ellen nodded her agreement as she eyed a particularly colorful painting of a waterfall cascading into a bluish green lagoon, red and orange water lilies dotting its sparkling surface.

"Um, guys, you ready? Abigail just buzzed us in." Nick called from the lobby desk.

The trio made their way to a set of thick, richly varnished doors stained in a deep mahogany. Nick reached out and pulled the right door open, beckoning Ellen and Scott through first.

"You must be Ellen." A trim woman in her early fifties said as she extended a perfectly manicured hand. "I'm Abigail."

Ellen smiled politely and shook the older woman's hand, noticing the array of shiny diamonds that adorned her fingers. "Pleased to meet you. This is my husband, Scott."

Abigail briefly paused, a smile playing on her crimson lips. "My, aren't you a handsome fellow."

Scott blushed slightly but took the woman's outstretched hand and gave it a gentle shake. "Hello. Thanks for seeing us."

"My pleasure." The woman said, her eyes quickly focusing on Nick.

Nick came forward and lightly embraced the woman. "Abigail, so good to see you again. I can't tell you how much I appreciate you seeing us on such short notice."

Abigail batted her eyes ever so demurely and gave Nick an award-winning smile. "Oh, dear, I never pass up the opportunity to speak with a colleague. Especially one that might harbor a news breaking story." And with a mischievous gleam in her eye, Abigail led them to her office.

Her office was oversized and plush. An expensive looking wool rug covered dark wood floors. Velvet drapes in a deep plum color adorned the windows. A massive mahogany desk sat near the window. A sitting area off to the left was made up of two grey leather armchairs and a matching leather sofa tastefully scattered with throw pillows. A colorful giclee centered above the sofa hung on the wall. Finally, on the opposite wall were floor to ceiling bookcases filled with leatherbound books.

Nick let out a low whistle and said, "I'm obviously working for the wrong paper".

Smiling, Abigail indicated they should make themselves comfortable. Rather than sitting behind her impressive desk, Abigail chose instead to sit in one of the two leather chairs. Nick took the other which left the sofa for Ellen and Scott.

"Would you care for anything to drink?" Abigail asked. Everyone shook their heads no so she continued. "Very well. What can I do for you today? Nick mentioned you had some information regarding the Emily Garritson case?"

Nick jumped in before Ellen or Scott could say anything. "Well, Abigail, I may not have been completely forthcoming about our visit."

Abigail scoffed and said, "Honestly, Nick, I figured as much. You don't get to be where I am without learning a thing or two about the ways of the world. So what really brings you to see me?" She asked, leveling her gaze on Ellen.

Ellen looked at Scott and he squeezed her hand reassuringly. "Well, it's kind of a long story but here goes…" and Ellen relayed everything to this woman she had just met. She left out no detail no matter how small or seemingly insignificant.

When Ellen was finished relaying her story, Abigail sat looking at her with her head slightly tilted and a pensive look on her face. "Well that's quite a story." She said as she got up and began pacing and mulling over what she had just been told.

"Did you ever suspect the two cases were connected?" Ellen wanted to know.

Abigail stopped pacing and said, "I have to be very clear here. I did suspect there was a link but I can't take all the credit. I had an unexpected source that..."she paused to think of the right way to put it, "may have given me some information."

"Who?" Nick asked.

"I guess there's no harm in revealing it now." Abigail said, shaking her head sadly. "It was Emily herself."

Chapter 28

You could have heard a pin drop after Abigail revealed Emily was her source. Ellen, Scott and Nick just sat there, waiting expectantly for Abigail to offer further explanation.

Looking at Ellen, Abigail said, "That's why you found the newspaper articles in your daughter's room. Emily hid them there prior to her death. She had been collecting the articles trying to find an explanation for Jenny's disappearance."

Mulling this over, Scott spoke up first. "If Emily came to you about Jenny's disappearance, didn't you think it was a little coincidental when she was killed?"

"Of course I did, Mr. Christiansen. But you have to understand, I believed that Morton Sullivan was behind Emily's death." Abigail said by way of an explanation.

"But surely you looked into it?" Nick asked.

Abigail narrowed her gaze and said, "I wouldn't be a very good journalist if I hadn't. I discreetly opened my own investigation, but it led nowhere. Not to mention, the evidence pointing to Morton Sullivan's guilt was pretty compelling." Abigail concluded.

Ellen mulled this over before saying, "Did Emily give any indication who she thought was behind Jenny's disappearance?"

Abigail shook her head and said, "Sadly, no. She was really just starting to look into it and was gathering facts. She only came to me because she thought, since I wrote a lot of the articles, I would have more information than what was printed. The last time we spoke Emily was excited and said she was getting closer to the truth but that's all she said. She never gave me a name."

"So it's possible that Emily mentioned her suspicions to the killer and eluded she was getting close to the truth so he or she killed her." Scott concluded.

"And then, by a stroke of luck for our killer, the police zeroed in on Morton Sullivan because of his checkered past and the killer seized the opportunity and framed Morton." Nick chimed in.

"It all sounds plausible, but you are going to need a lot more than supposition to get the police to take you seriously." Abigail pointed out.

Nick stood up and said, "She's right. We need to find out who Emily talked to or how the killer knew she was looking into the Jenny Mathews case."

"But how can we possibly know who she talked to?" Ellen asked, frustration tinging her words.

"What about her boyfriend at the time?" Nick asked.

"Toby?" Abigail asked and then gave a dismissive wave. "It wasn't him. He was a nice enough boy and really took Emily's death hard but, not to sound insulting, he just wasn't bright enough to pull off such a complex crime."

"We need to start interviewing everyone that knew Emily and see if we can link anyone to the crime." Nick said.

Scott jumped in, "Okay but we really need to be careful. We think this person killed two young girls so there's nothing to suggest he or she won't do the same to one of us if we get too close to the truth."

They all nodded their agreement and decided the best place to start was talking to the school to find out who Emily's friends were. Perhaps she had confided in a girlfriend or even a school counselor. They agreed to get back together over the weekend to discuss their findings. Ellen and Scott said their goodbyes and headed out while Nick remained behind to chat some more with Abigail.

Back in the car, Ellen breathed a sigh of relief. It felt as if things were starting to move in the right direction and she was getting closer to figuring out what was going on in her house. She just needed a few more days to piece things together. If she could figure out what happened to Jenny then she could finally put this all behind her and focus on the future with her family.

....

Later that evening, Ellen and Scott took a break from sleuthing and invited Marcie over to play board games with Natalie. While Scott whipped up some buffalo chicken dip, Ellen and Marcie made milk shakes. After the snacks were prepared, they all sat down at the kitchen table to play Candyland.

"My God this shake is heaven!" Marcie said smiling contentedly.

Natalie giggled and pointed at Marcie who had a very noticeable milkshake mustache above her upper lip.

"What are you laughing at, kiddo?" Marcie asked.

Ellen burst out laughing and said, "You may want to take a look in a mirror."

Marcie pulled a compact out of her purse and checked her reflection. She then snatched up a napkin from the table and swiped it across her mouth. "You guys just don't know how to appreciate a good milkshake." She told them and chuckled good heartedly.

They continued joking with one another as they played and enjoyed their shakes and dip. Everyone's spirits were high and the night passed by quickly. After a while, Natalie started yawning. Scott glanced at his watch and said, "Okay, Nat, I think it's time to get you to bed."

Natalie protested and insisted she wasn't tired but couldn't stifle another yawn. Laughing, Scott picked her up and told her to say goodnight. The little girl begrudgingly agreed and said goodnight. Ellen and Marcie stood up and gave her a kiss on each cheek then Scott carried her upstairs.

As soon as the coast was clear, Ellen began filling Marcie in on their meeting with Abigail. By the time she finished, Scott came back into the kitchen. "What did I miss?" he wanted to know.

"I was just telling Marcie what happened with Abigail." Ellen explained.

Marcie said "Well at least we know why the articles were hidden in Natalie's closet. What I don't understand, though, is what got Emily's curiosity piqued to begin with?"

"That's a good question." Ellen said. "To be honest, I've been so caught up in figuring out who the killer was I didn't even think about why Emily started looking into

Jenny's disappearance in the first place. Maybe she found the locket?"

Scott nodded thoughtfully and said, "It's possible. Just because the locket was hidden in the basement when you found it doesn't mean that's where Emily found it."

"Good point. We need to find someone who was close to Emily at the time that she may have confided in." Ellen stated.

"Are you going to try and talk to Toby?" Marcie asked.

Shaking her head Ellen said, "I haven't been able to track him down since he moved and, besides, I think it's more likely Emily confided in a close girlfriend. I remember being that age and there was nothing I wouldn't tell my friends."

"How are you going to find out who Emily's friends were?" Marcie wanted to know.

"I think it's time we pay another visit to the high school. Hopefully someone will remember Emily and maybe we can get our hands on some old yearbooks or something else that will help us figure out who Emily was close to." Ellen concluded.

Dipping the last chip into the now cold buffalo chicken dip Marcie said, "Well you can count me in. When are we going?"

"It's time to put an end to this. We're going to go first thing in the morning." Ellen said.

....

The next morning, Scott left for work and Ellen dropped Natalie off at daycare then met Marcie for an early breakfast at JD's Diner, a local mom and & pop restaurant that, despite a bland décor, served the best hash browns around.

The waitress, a portly woman in her late 40s with a bad dye job and eye make-up that would require a chisel to remove, took their order without looking at them then sauntered back to the kitchen. As she walked away, her perfume hung in the air like an unwanted guest.

"If I ever become that jaded, please shoot me." Marcie said as she added six packets of sugar to her coffee.

"Do you like a little coffee with your sugar?" Ellen asked, joking.

Smiling, Marcie replied, "It's the only way I can drink the stuff." Changing the subject, she then asked, "So what's the game plan for today?"

"Well, I think we head straight to the school office and see if anyone remembers Emily." Ellen answered.

"Are we going in with a cover story or…what?" Marcie asked.

Ellen considered this. "I think we tell the truth. I live in the house Emily used to live in and I came across some of her things and wanted to find out more about her."

"Okay. What do you think the odds are that someone still works at the school who will remember Emily or her friends?" Marcie wanted to know.

Before Ellen could answer, their unenthusiastic waitress returned with their breakfast. Wordlessly, she sat the plates down then unceremoniously slipped the check under Ellen's plate and walked away.

Marcie looked at Ellen then shrugged and turned her attention to her behemoth plate of extra crispy bacon, two eggs over medium, hash browns covered in cheese, and French toast. Ellen watched as Marcie drizzled half a bottle of maple syrup over her French toast, used her fork to saw off a huge chunk, then shoveled it into her mouth. Looking down at her own plate of egg whites and wheat toast, Ellen wondered for the thousandth time how Marcie managed to maintain a size 2 figure while eating more food than most Olympic athletes.

After they finished breakfast and paid, they both hopped into Ellen's car and drove in

the direction of Crescentville High. Traffic
was lighter than usual so they made good time,
arriving at the school just before 8am.

Nestled between the football field and a
huge, wooded lot, Crescentville High sat
stoically, flanked by two huge Blue Spruce
trees, atop a small slope. The sun reflected off
the school's windows, momentarily blinding
Ellen as she pulled into the lot. Because the
school year had already ended, only a few cars
speckled the recently paved parking lot.

Pulling the car into a space closest to the
front entrance, the two ladies gathered their
belongings and made their way up the stairs to
the school's front entrance. A huge metal
sculpture, someone's idea of art, sat smack dab
in the middle of the front entrance of the school.
As the two women passed by the obtrusive
sculpture, they couldn't help but notice the art
piece had been the victim of blatant vandalism.
The message, a red spray-painted affront to the
sculpture's otherwise pristine white surface,
read *"Tammy is a slut"*.

"I wonder who Tammy is?" Marcie
asked.

"I don't know but I feel bad for her."
Ellen replied as she opened the right side of the
glass double doors.

The two women walked into a wide
entry. The original floors were hardwood and in

remarkably good condition considering the school was built in the 70s. A pale, minty green tile ran halfway up the walls and, above that, the walls were painted the same pale minty green color. Framed color photos adorned the wall, the subjects of the photos presumably past students and staff. Straight ahead were a pair of wooden double doors and hallways veered off to the right and left of the entry.

"Where to?" Marcie asked.

Ellen glanced at the wooden doors and opened one of them to reveal a darkened gymnasium inside. Having been there not long before, she turned to the right and said, "This way."

Glancing left then right, a light could be seen spilling out of one of the doorways about midway down the hallway to the right. In unison, Ellen and Marcie began walking in that direction, their footsteps echoing softly off the metal lockers that lined the hallway on both sides.

Knocking gently on the door frame to announce their presence, Ellen and Marcie stepped into a large room that was the school office. A huge wood desk wrapped halfway around the room. On the wall behind the desk, rows of wooden cubby holes hung for mail and other important paperwork. Each cubby was labeled with a name underneath. Off to the left was a hallway that led to Principle Turner's. There were some chairs and a small table that made up a waiting area. Magazines were fanned out on the table's surface to keep waiting guests entertained until they could be seen. A water cooler was nestled in the corner with small paper cups sitting next to it.

"May I help you?" an older woman in her early 70s asked as she emerged from the hallway. She was thin and slightly stooped and wore a floral print dress that was cinched at the waist with a wide patent leather belt. Her gray hair was cut short with stylish curls sprayed neatly into place. Cat eyeglasses hung from a chain around her neck and she pulled them on as she approached Ellen and Marcie. The glasses magnified her eyes, giving her an owl-like appearance. She had not been here during Ellen's last visit.

"Hi." Ellen began, extending her hand. "My name is Ellen and this is my friend Marcie. We were hoping to talk to someone who may have known a student that used to go here."

The woman smiled and introduced herself. "I'm Blanche Hughes, the school secretary. I've been here since 1983. Unfortunately, no one else is here so you're stuck with me. Please, have a seat." She indicated the chairs in the small waiting area.

"Thank you, Mrs. Hughes." Ellen said as she took a seat in one of the chairs.

"It's Miss, actually, but you can just call me Blanche. Can I get either of you some coffee or hot chocolate?"

Politely, both women declined and waited for Blanche to take a seat as well. "What can I do for you?"

"We were wondering if you knew a student named Emily Garritson?" Ellen asked.

Blanche shook her head sadly and said, "Yes I remember Emily. A tragedy what happened to her. Are you two reporters?"

"No." Ellen said emphatically. "I actually moved into the house that Emily lived in. The one on Owl Creek." She added, although she wasn't sure if that part was important.

"Oh, I see." Said Blanche. "Well, what would you like to know about Emily?"

Ellen looked at Marcie who nodded reassuringly so Ellen said, "Anything you can tell us really. I found some old photos and newspaper clippings in my house and I just wanted to try and find out more about Emily and what happened to her. I thought maybe someone here at the school could maybe put me in touch with some of Emily's friends perhaps?"

"Emily worked as an aide in the school office so I got to know her, although she was a quiet girl. Very smart, mind you, and well-behaved. She was sweet as well. Maybe a little nosy-but not in a bad way." Blanche was quick to tell them.

"What do you mean by nosy?" Marcie asked.

Blanche considered this for a moment before answering, "I mean like she considered herself a bit of a detective...like Nancy Drew." She added, smiling.

"So she was curious about things and launched her own investigations?" Ellen wanted to know.

"Yes but she did it in a way that you may not catch on right away that's what she was up to." Blanche recalled.

Ellen thought about this before asking, "Did Emily have any friends you can recall?"

Blanche nodded and said, "Yes she had a couple of close girlfriends. She was well-liked but not really popular but more like by choice. She had a boyfriend also. He was a nice boy and came from a good family."

Ellen scooted closer to the edge of her seat, hopeful she would learn something promising. "We know about the boyfriend, Toby, but do you recall the names of her girlfriends and do you know if they still live in the area?"

"I may be old but my mind is still sharp as a tack." Blanche said with a wink. "She was friends with Marie Stephens and Gabby Dodge. I know that Marie went off to college and I'm afraid I lost track of her but Gabby still lives in town. In fact, she worked at the Library the last I heard."

"That's so helpful Blanche. Thank you so much." Ellen told the older woman as she and Marcie stood up to leave.

"You are so very welcome, dear. It was nice to sit and talk and reminisce a little." Blanche said smiling. "If you want to leave your number with me, I will be happy to see what else I can dig up and give you a call if I find anything worth mentioning."

Ellen quickly jotted her number down on a post it note and handed it to the woman. "Once again, thank you so much for everything."

The two women exited the building and made a beeline for the car. "What now?" Marcie wanted to know as she buckled the seatbelt around her slender waist.

"Well I have to get to work. Andrew has been very understanding about everything but I can't keep missing. It's not fair to him." Ellen said as she started the car and began backing out of the parking space.

"I totally understand, Ell. I never stopped to think how all of this was impacting your life. I have just been so caught up in figuring it all out..." Marcie said, her voice trailing off as tears formed in her big blue eyes.

"Oh Marcie!" Ellen said, throwing the car into park. "It's okay. You aren't the only one that has been caught up, trust me. I want to figure this all out too. I honestly don't think I could have gotten through all this without you. Now come here, you blubbering fool." Ellen said as she reached her arms out to embrace her friend.

The two women sat that way for a few minutes, crying and hugging. Slowly, the tears subsided and they regained their composure.

Ellen looked at Marcie as she gently blotted her eyes with a fast-food napkin that was stashed in the cup holder. "Is my mascara running?"

Despite everything, Marcie and Ellen both burst out laughing. "Let's go." Marcie told her friend once her giggles quieted. "If you want, I can try to track down Gabby while you are at work?"

"That would be a huge help!" Ellen exclaimed, genuinely touched by her friend's willingness to help out.

"No problem. Drop me off at my car and I will call you if I find out anything." Marcie said.

The two women parted ways a short time later and Ellen headed into the office, determined to concentrate on her work and not allow everything happening at her house to distract her. She felt like she was getting closer to the truth. She only hoped she wouldn't pay the same price Emily and Jenny paid.

....

Later that afternoon, Marcie called Ellen to report that she went by the Library and, although Gabby Dodge still worked there, she was not at work today. Marcie also let Ellen know she was able to pry Gabby's home address out of one of Gabby's coworkers at the library and was planning on heading over there but wanted to know if Ellen wanted to join her after she got off work.

After thinking about it for a few seconds, Ellen decided she would like to go with Marcie. She told Marcie to meet her at the office after work then sent a quick text to Scott to see if he was okay with the plan. He responded almost immediately and gave her the okay.

Work was busy and the day passed by in a blur. Ellen sat in on two depositions, both pertaining to an upcoming trial for a case involving tax fraud. After the depositions, she typed up several briefs while eating lunch at her desk. She then spent the afternoon researching environmental laws and then gathered all her research into a file for Andrew to review in the morning.

Fully immersed in her work, Ellen barely noticed as the office cleared out. It wasn't until Tucker Whitt, a summer intern, stopped by her desk and asked if she wanted him to walk her out to her car.

Barely glancing up she said, "Thanks for offering but I will be leaving in just a few minutes. I'll see you tomorrow."

Ellen looked at her watch and saw it was 5:20pm. She realized she should wrap things up here at work as Marcie would be arriving any minute. She quickly logged off her computer then made a quick stop at the lady's restroom. After using the toilet, she washed her hands and ran a brush through her hair.

Tossing a final look in the mirror, she grabbed the handle to open the bathroom door but the door remained stubbornly closed. Puzzled, Ellen tried opening the door again but it was useless. Ellen started banging on the door but remembered everyone else had left for the day.

Alarm started to set in but Ellen pushed it back and tried to think of a plan to get out of the bathroom. She unzipped her purse and began searching its contents, looking for her phone. After pulling everything out of her purse, she remembered her phone was sitting on her desk, plugged into the charger. She had wanted to make sure it was fully charged in case she and Marcie got lost on their way to Gabby's.

Damn.

Next, Ellen looked around the bathroom, trying to locate something she could use to maybe try and pry the door open. Scanning the small room, Ellen quickly rejected the idea of being able to pry the door open. The only items in the bathroom consisted of a built in sink, a paper towel dispenser, hand soap, toilet and a waste basket.

She was just on the verge of attempting to hoist herself up on the sink to inspect the sprinkler system when the bathroom lights suddenly went out, plunging the room into complete darkness.

The alarm bells Ellen had managed to quiet just a few minutes earlier now began to ring loud and urgently. She tried to remain calm, telling herself it was just bad luck that she had locked herself in the bathroom and now the lights had gone off. They were probably on a timer. She had almost convinced herself this was true when she heard the distinct sound of footsteps outside the bathroom door.

"Hello?" She called out, hopeful it was Marcie or Tucker or the cleaning lady.

Silence was the only answer she received. As she listened, she could hear the hum from the refrigerator in the breakroom but nothing else.

"Is anyone there?" She asked again.

Again, she was greeted by silence. She was beginning to convince herself that she had imagined the footsteps when a voice whispered, "Stop putting your nose where it doesn't belong or you're going to end up like Emily."

Fear raced through Ellen's veins, and she stumbled backwards into the wall. She slowly slid down the wall and pulled her knees to her chest. Tears stung her eyes and her stomach heaved as bile raced up her throat.

As the first tears began to run down her cheeks, Ellen heard footsteps and a woman's voice calling out her name. Marcie!

Jumping to her feet, Ellen yelled, "I'm locked in the bathroom! Help me!"

"Ell?" Marcie asked from outside the bathroom door. "How'd you manage to lock yourself in the bathroom?"

Relief surged through Ellen as the door unlocked and light from the hallway came streaming in. Ellen ran forward and threw her arms around Marcie. "We have to call the police. Someone was here. They locked me in the bathroom and threatened me." Ellen explained as she pulled Marcie down the hall and towards the front door.

"Ellen wait. Are you saying someone was here? Just now?" Marcie asked.

"Yes! That's exactly what I'm saying. We have to get out of here." Ellen said, again heading for the door.

"Who was it?" Marcie asked as she followed Ellen outside.

Remembering her cell phone was still inside, Ellen asked Marcie to call the police. After the call was placed, she explained everything that happened to her friend, careful not to leave out any details.

"Oh my God. This is really serious." Marcie said.

As sirens sounded in the distance, Ellen looked at her friend and, in a shaky voice, said, "I know Marcie. What have we gotten ourselves into?"

Chapter 29

"Let me get this straight," Deputy Daniel Riggs was saying as he chewed the tip of his pen, "You didn't actually see anyone?"

Standing at least an inch shorter than her, Ellen guessed his weight at a 140lbs tops. Despite being in his early 20s, his reddish-brown hair was already receding and the mustache he was attempting to grow was made up of patchy puffs of peach fuzz. It was difficult to take him seriously, let alone feel confident in his ability to figure out who was behind this recent threat on her life. Ellen sighed loudly, despite her best efforts to control her frustration, and taking a deep breath to steady her voice, she responded matter-of-factly. "Yes that's exactly what I am saying. But, as I already told you, I HEARD someone."

Deputy Riggs looked up sharply from his notepad. "I am just trying to understand what happened here ma'am. No need to take a tone with me." He said as he tucked the small spiral notepad in the chest pocket of his tan and brown deputy issued shirt.

"She's just been through a major scare so cut her some slack." Marcie piped up.

At the sound of her voice, Deputy Riggs appeared to noticeable swoon before their very eyes. "I didn't mean anything by it." He said as he ogled Marcie dreamily.

"Can we leave now?" Ellen asked, all attempts at being civil going out the window. Her patience was run thin. She was scared, confused and hungry which made for a lethal combination.

Bristling, Deputy Riggs cleared his throat and said, "Yes. I have your statements. I will let you know if I find anything."

The words had barely left his mouth before Ellen was grabbing her phone off her desk and heading for the door, pulling Marcie behind her.

"Is incompetence a requirement to work on the police force around her?" Ellen asked once they were outside and safely out of earshot.

Marcie couldn't help but laugh then added, "He was just young. Besides, we've got bigger fish to fry. Obviously, we are getting close to the truth or whoever locked you in that bathroom and threatened you wouldn't have taken such a risky chance. I mean, how could he or she have known you would be alone?"

Marcie had a point. It did appear they were closing in on the killer. "You may be right. Do you still want to go to Gabby's? It's almost 8pm." Ellen said glancing at her watch. She had called Scott about an hour earlier and although he wanted to come down to the office to be with her, she had insisted he keep Natalie at home. The last thing she wanted was for Natalie to see the police dusting her office for prints.

"I don't think we have a choice." Marcie said. "But do you care if we grab something to eat on the way? I'm starving."

Ellen chuckled and said, "That sounds like a good idea. I'm hungry myself and we need all the strength we can get if we're going to figure this all out."

....

Forty-five minutes later, an empty fast-food bag between them, Ellen and Marcie sat across the street from Gabby Dodge's house. The cute little Cape Cod was located on a well-lit street tucked behind the Save-A-Lot grocery store. Though small, the house was neatly maintained, the yard recently cut with red petunias lining the walkway and ferns hanging from the porch eaves. A well-trimmed Rose of Sharon was the centerpiece of the yard.

"Should we just walk up and knock?" Marcie asked as she glanced into the empty fast-food bag, hoping she had missed a stray fry.

"Yeah. At this point, we don't have time to mess around. Let's get this over with." Ellen said, unbuckling her seatbelt and opening her car door.

Making their way up to the front door, Ellen was about to knock when the door swung open. Startled, Ellen and Marcie jumped back.

A woman stood in the doorway, the light from behind her spilling out onto the porch and illuminating the encroaching darkness of the night. She was petite and slight, her dark brown hair pulled back from her face into a low ponytail, emphasizing her high cheekbones. Almond shaped eyes, the color of black coffee stared kindly at Ellen and Marcie. "May I help you?" She asked in a voice both strong and melodic.

Ellen took a few steps forward and asked, "Are you Gabby?"

The woman nodded and smiled so Ellen continued. "Hello. My name is Ellen, and this is my friend Marcie. We're so sorry to bother you so late but we got your name from Blanche over at the high school. We were hoping to speak with you about Emily."

Gabby moved to the side, holding the door open and indicating Ellen and Marcie should come in. "Please have a seat. Would you like something to drink?"

Ellen and Marcie sat down at a small round, white kitchen table while Gabby busied herself making a drink. Glancing around, Ellen noticed the house was small but cozy. Everything was meticulously tidy and well-decorated.

Gabby returned to the table carrying a bottle of Bourbon and three glasses. She poured three finger's worth of the caramel liquid into each glass then added another splash for good measure. She swept her hand towards the glasses indicating they should each take one. "So why are you asking about Emily?"

Clearing her throat Ellen said, "You were her friend, right?"

Nodding, Gabby's eyes took on a faraway look as she no doubt thought back to her high school days. "Yes, she was my best friend I would say. We were incredibly close and had been since second grade when Jimmy Reynolds threw a spider at Emily, and I hit him with a roll of Kraft paper." She chucked at the memory and took a long swallow from her glass.

"I moved into her old house…on Owl Creek Street." Ellen explained. "I honestly am too exhausted to beat around the bush so I'm just going to cut straight to the chase. I think my house is haunted by a girl named Jenny Matthews and somehow Emily is connected. Tonight, someone locked me in a bathroom and threatened me so I am worried me and my family may be in danger. I have to find out what happened."

"Emily always had a nose for a story. She loved solving mysteries and figuring out the killer in a those whodunnit books she always had her face buried in. She was sweet and kind and funny and…" Gabby stopped momentarily as her eyes filled up with tears and she got up to grab a tissue off a built-in shelf behind the sofa.

"Did you know she was looking into the disappearance of Jenny Matthews?" Ellen asked kindly.

Gabby nodded. "Yes. It was all she could talk about those last few weeks leading up to her death. She was convinced that Jenny had been killed. She said she could feel it and she was determined to find out who did it."

"Did she?" Ellen asked. "Find out who did it, I mean?"

"I don't know but she was definitely on the trail and the last I heard she was trying to track down a boy that mowed the grass at one of the houses down the street from where Jenny's grandparents lived." Gabby said, taking a gulp of her bourbon and wincing slightly as the strong liquid hit the back of her throat.

"Do you remember who it was? Was it Josh Masterson?" Ellen asked, scooting forward on her chair. This could be the break they were looking for.

Shaking her head, Gabby said, "No I would remember if it was Josh. He was friends with Emily's brother and a real pain in everyone's ass, but he wasn't the one Emily was trying to find. It's been a long time though and I just can't seem to recall his name."

"It's okay." Marcie said, placing her hand on the woman's arm reassuringly. "It may come back to you."

Gabby nodded sadly and said, "I think about her a lot you know? She was so full of life; I can't help but wonder where she would be right now if she was still alive."

Ellen nodded and asked, "If I give you my number, will you call me if you remember anything else?"

"Of course. I apologize for getting all choked up. It's just that I have never had another friend like Emily you know. She was one-of-a-kind. Anyway, yes, if you leave your number with me, I will give you a call if I think of anything."

Getting up, Ellen and Marcie explained they needed to get going but thanked the woman for the drinks and for talking with them and promised to keep her informed if they learned anything about either Jenny or Emily's deaths.

Back in the car, Marcie said, "How are we ever going to find the name of a boy who used to mow the lawn of one of Jenny's grandparent's neighbors when we don't even know which house it was?"

"I agree it's not much to go on but at least it's something new." Ellen remarked as she put the car into drive and headed in the direction of her office to drop Marcie off at her car.

Once she had dropped Marcie off, Ellen stopped by the store and picked up microwave popcorn and Milk Duds. She figured she wasn't going to sleep well with what happened at the office so she might as well stay up late watching movies and eating junk food.

Just as she was pulling into her driveway, her phone rang. Looking at the screen she saw it was Andrew. "Hello." She answered.

"Hi Ellen. I'm so glad I caught you. I just got off the phone with the police. Are you okay?" Andrew asked, his voice tinged with worry.

"Oh my God Andrew! I meant to call you earlier and fill you in but just got caught up with everything that happened. I'm fine though I promise." She assured her boss.

"Okay. Just so you know I closed the office for the next couple of days. I don't want anyone there after what happened. At least not until the police can assure me that it's safe." Andrew explained.

Ellen felt horrible. Now her boss was losing out on billable hours because of her. "You don't have to do that Andrew. I'm sure everyone knows this wasn't your fault and it was just a random onetime thing."

"That may be but better safe than sorry. Besides, I have court most of the week anyway. And whatever I do need done outside of the courtroom, I'm sure we can manage from home, okay?" He asked.

"Okay thank you Andrew. And, again, I'm sorry I didn't call you sooner." Ellen said as she hung up the phone.

Grabbing her purse and the bag of snacks she headed into the house. She had a feeling it was going to be a long night.

....

The next morning, Ellen woke up early despite a restless night of sleep. She was anxious to finish working on some details on a file she had brought home from work. She knew Andrew would need it for later in the week. Scott and Natalie were still asleep, so Ellen made her way downstairs quietly.

In the kitchen, she started the coffee maker and looked in the fridge for something she could make for breakfast. Deciding on toast and fruit, Ellen set about preparing her breakfast. By the time she had finished the coffee was done so she poured herself a mug of the dark blend and added a little cream.

Sitting down at the table, she opened her laptop and started working on the file for work. She quickly became engrossed in her work and barely noticed when Boo sauntered into the kitchen and quietly eased himself into her lap. She absently scratched behind his ear while she ate her breakfast and read over the file.

A short time later, Scott came downstairs followed by a wide-eyed Natalie. "What are you doing up so early?" Scott asked as he grabbed the jug of orange juice from the fridge and poured a glass for himself and Natalie.

"I couldn't sleep so I figured I might as well get some work done." Ellen explained.

Scott came up behind Ellen and put his hands on her shoulders. "Do you want me to stay home with you today?"

Ellen had filled her husband in on everything last night when she had finally returned home, and she had also let him know she would be working from home for today and possibly the remainder of the week. "No honey. Honestly, I'm fine and, besides, I really do have a lot of work to do, and I can probably accomplish more if I don't have any distractions. Thank you for offering though."

She added as she kissed his right hand that rested on her shoulder.

"I get it. Say no more. I will leave you alone but promise to call me if anything happens, okay?" He asked.

She promised him she would and offered to take Natalie to daycare but Scott insisted he would drive the little girl so Ellen could get some work done.

After they had gone for the day, Ellen became lost in her work and, before long, she looked up from her laptop and saw that it was already nearly 12:30. She couldn't believe how much time had passed! She decided to take a bathroom break and then make herself lunch.

After using the bathroom, she busied herself in the kitchen making a grilled chicken salad with cherry tomatoes, sliced carrots, feta cheese and croutons. She topped it off with a creamy honey mustard vinaigrette dressing. She also made herself a tall glass of iced tea.

Carrying everything back to the kitchen table, she was just about to dig in when her cell phone began vibrating on the table. She didn't recognize the number, so she hesitated to answer but finally hit the talk button. "Hello?"

"Hi Ellen?" A female voice asked.

"Yes, this is she." Ellen told the woman on the other end of the line.

"I'm so glad I caught you. This is Gabby. You know, Emily's friend? Anyway, I told you I would call if I thought of anything else?"

Ellen sat up straighter, hopeful the woman was calling with some information that could finally help her figure out all the strange events surrounding her house. "Hi Gabby, I didn't expect to hear from you so soon. So, what did you remember?" Ellen asked. She could barely keep the excitement out of her voice.

"So, I couldn't stop thinking about Emily after you left. Finally, in the middle of the night I woke up and remembered the name of the boy Emily was going to interview. You know, the one I told you mowed grass in Jenny's neighborhood?" Gabby explained.

"Yes, I remember…" Ellen said, waiting expectantly for Gabby to reveal his name.

"It was Stephen Mitchem." Gabby said, sounding somewhat triumphant.

Ellen pondered this new information. "Do you know if he still lives around here?"

"I don't know actually. I vaguely remember him from school. He was quiet, kept to himself. Never really talked much and didn't have a lot of friends as I recall. I think he only attended Crescentville High for a year or two and then I assume he moved or transferred schools. I honestly don't remember what happened to him." Gabby said.

Mulling over this new information Ellen thanked Gabby and hung up the phone. Stephen Mitchem. The name didn't sound familiar, so it was not someone she had come across before.

She tried calling Scott, but it went straight to voicemail. Next, she called Marcie, but it rang three times then her voicemail picked up. Leaving a message for them both, Ellen decided she would finish up with her work and then spend the evening trying to figure out who Stephen Mitchem was and if he still lived in the area.

....

Later that evening, after dinner, Scott asked if Ellen minded if he went bowling for a few hours. "I'm so sorry for the late notice." He explained. "I honestly forgot I signed up for the league a few weeks ago and tonight is the first match. If you don't want me to go though, just say the word."

Ellen smiled reassuringly at her husband. Ever since he joined Team Ellen regarding the weird events surrounding their house, Scott had been very supportive. He deserved to have a little fun every now and then. "I want you to go. You have worked so hard and done so much for me lately, I want you to go and have a good time and I don't want to hear another word about it." She told him, putting her arms around his neck and kissing him.

"Okay, if you are sure. Like I said, I should only be gone a few hours tops. If you need me for anything, I'll have my cell phone on." He told her then headed upstairs to change his clothes and grab his bowling ball from the hall closet.

Kissing Ellen and Natalie goodbye, Scott headed out the door. Moments later Ellen heard his car pulling out of the drive.

Turning to Natalie, she asked, "What do you want to do tonight kiddo?"

"Can we play zoo?" Natalie asked. She had a small toy zoo with animals and lifelike habitats.

"Sure, but only if I can be the Chimpanzee." Ellen said, jumping up and making monkey noises as she helped Natalie set up the game on the living room floor.

An hour later, Ellen noticed Natalie couldn't stop yawning. "Come on, Nat. Let's brush our teeth and get ready for bed, okay?"

They made their way upstairs and Ellen helped Natalie brush her teeth. Afterwards, she snuggled into Natalie's bed with her and read to her until the little girl fell into a peaceful sleep. Ellen slowly eased out of the bed, careful not to disturb Natalie and made her way back downstairs.

Just as she poured herself a glass of wine and was getting ready to curl up on the couch and try to find out anything she could about Stephen Mitchem, her cell phone chirped. Glancing at the caller ID, she saw it was Marcie. "Hi Marcie. I tried calling you earlier, but I take it you had a busy day."

"I did. Jesse and I were buried neck deep in plans for the business. What's up?" Marcie asked.

"I got a call earlier from Gabby. She remembered the name of that boy she mentioned when we were at her house last night." Ellen explained.

"You mean the one that mowed lawns in Jenny's neighborhood?" Marcie asked.

"One and the same. She said it was a boy by the name of Stephen Mitchem. She didn't really have any more information about him though and I haven't had a chance to investigate him yet. I've been busy with work and then Scott went bowling tonight so I was playing a game with Natalie until she went to bed just a little while ago. Anyway, your timing is perfect because I literally just sat down to see what I could find out." Ellen told her friend as she grabbed her laptop from the kitchen and brought it into the living room.

"I'm already on it." Marcie said and Ellen could hear her clicking away on the keyboard as she apparently Googled Stephen Mitchem to see what she could uncover. "Do we know if he still lives in the area?" She asked.

"I honestly don't know. Gabby mentioned that he kind of disappeared from high school and she never really knew what happened but assumed he moved away." Ellen explained.

"Okay, well I'm on Facebook right now and there's a Stephen Mitchem that lives in the area, at least according to his profile." Marcie said.

"That could be him. Is he about the right age?" Ellen wanted to know.

"Uh yeah. That's an affirmative. Looks like he's not in a relationship, he's a Virgo and likes fishing…." Marcie said absently as she perused Stephen's Facebook page.

Ellen noticed the battery on her phone was almost dead, so she started searching for her charging cable while she waited for Marcie to dig up something useful. She searched the kitchen where she usually kept her charger, but it was missing from its usual place. Scott had probably grabbed it on his way out.

"Find anything else?" Ellen asked Marcie as she rummaged noisily through the junk drawer in search of a spare cable.

"Give me a sec. He's got all kinds of privacy settings which is making it more difficult to uncover anything helpful." Marcie said absently.

Ellen was just about to head upstairs to search for her charger up there when the house was plunged into darkness. "Dammit!" she said, stubbing her toe on the bottom stair.

"What is it?" Marcie asked.

"I think the power just went out." Ellen explained as she turned the flashlight feature on her cell phone on. Just as it illuminated the path in front of her, the cell phone gave one last chirp and then the battery died, shutting the flashlight off in the process. Ellen was once again plunged into darkness.

Before she could start making her way down the hallway towards the kitchen where the spare flashlight was kept, Ellen heard the floor creak behind her. "Natalie, honey, is that you?" Ellen said into the darkness.

No response. Ellen was beginning to think it had just been the cat when something grabbed her from behind. Before she knew what was happening, a damp rag was pressed over her mouth and nose, and she felt herself slipping towards unconsciousness. Her last thought before she blacked out was, *I'm going to end up just like Jenny and Emily.*

Chapter 30

Ellen awoke slowly. Her mind felt foggy, so it took her a moment to get her bearings. She slowly became aware that she was sitting in a chair and her hands were tied behind her. She also couldn't see. At first, she thought it was just the darkness that was causing her blindness, but she realized that she was blindfolded. She could feel the fabric pressed into her temples and forehead. Her memory came flooding back and she remembered talking to Marcie on the phone and then the power going out and finally someone grabbing her. But who?

A scraping sound nearby caused Ellen's heart to momentarily stop, and she sucked in an involuntary breath as fear took over.

"I see you're awake." A male voice said just a few feet in front of Ellen. She didn't recognize the voice.

"Who are you and where am I? I want you to untie me this instant!" Ellen demanded, her voice trembling. She willed her heartbeat to slow so she could maintain control. She needed to be as alert as possible if she was going to get out of this.

The man chuckled, clearly amused. "I know you're scared. I can hear it in your voice. Jenny and Emily were scared too."

Ellen felt a chill run down her spine. There was something in his voice that scared her to the very core. "What do you want?" She needed to get him talking so she could figure out a way to get herself untied. She slowly and carefully tried moving her hands. The ropes were tight but if she worked at them then just maybe she could get free.

"What do I want?" he asked, his tone becoming more agitated. "All I wanted was for you to leave well enough alone. But you had to keep digging, didn't you? And now you're going to force me to kill you."

Ellen willed herself to stay calm even as fear coursed through her veins. Taking a deep breath to steady her nerves, she asked, "But why did you do it? Why did you kill Jenny and then Emily? What could either of them possibly have done to you?"

For a moment, Ellen wasn't sure if he was going to answer but then he said, "Emily was just like you. Nosy. She just wouldn't stop looking into Jenny's disappearance. I tried to scare her off but when that didn't work…. She left me no choice…" he said, his voice trailing off.

"And Jenny?" Ellen asked, risking another attempt to loosen her restraints. She thought she felt a little give.

"Jenny was…my everything. I loved her." The man said, a dull ache in his voice.

"Love? How could you kill her if you loved her?" Ellen asked incredulously.

This seemed to anger the man because he closed the narrow gap between them in seconds and backhanded her hard across the left side of her face. The force of the blow all but knocked her over. "Don't mock me, you meddling bitch!" he shouted.

Ellen fought to remain conscious. The strike to her head nearly knocked her out. She could hear a ringing in her left ear and tasted blood in her mouth.

After a few moments passed, she quietly managed to say, "I'm not mocking you. I'm just trying to understand. You're obviously very smart. I mean, you've eluded police for two decades. I just don't understand why you killed Jenny if you loved her." Maybe if she could appeal to his ego, she could keep him talking long enough to save herself.

He seemed to calm down. When he spoke again, his tone was more even and less tense. "I saw Jenny for the first time that same summer she went missing. My mom had sent me to live with my uncle for a while after I got into some trouble at school. My uncle believed that hard work and discipline was all I needed to get back on track, so he forced me to get a job.

I started mowing lawns in the neighborhood Jenny lived in.

She was beautiful. I knew I had to find a way to get to know her, so I started following her. She didn't have any friends at first, so I watched her reading on her grandparent's front porch or walking to the corner store to buy herself a soda."

"Did you finally approach her?" Ellen asked, working furiously at loosening the ropes that kept her restrained to the chair. She was beginning to think the ropes were made of titanium.

"Not at first. I was happy to just watch her from a distance. But then she started hanging out with that low-life Eric Garritson and his delinquent friends. I knew I had to do something. I followed her to the library that night and, afterwards, I heard Eric ask her to go to a party with him. She said she couldn't because she had to be home soon, so Eric and his friend left, and Jenny started walking home. At the end of her street, she suddenly seemed to change her mind about going home and cut across the street. I stayed behind her, wanting to see where she was headed."

"Where did she end up?" Ellen asked. The more he talked, the more time she bought herself to get free.

"She went to Eric Garritson's house. I hid in some bushes and watched as she took a seat on a bench by the lake. I assumed she was waiting for Eric to come home. After a few minutes, I worked up the nerve to go over and talk to her. She recognized me from her grandparent's neighborhood and was friendly at first but when I told her I had followed her, she became confused…scared even. I tried to explain myself but the more I said, the more frightened she became. She started to turn away from me, so I grabbed her by the arm. That seemed to really scare her, and she started pulling away, struggling against my grasp. I just wanted to make her see there was nothing to be afraid of and that I loved her, but she wouldn't listen to me.

She suddenly broke free of my grasp and turned to run but must have tripped. She hit her head on a big root. I ran to her side, but she was unconscious and bleeding from her head. I looked around and finally saw the cellar doors. I ran over and they were unlocked so I dragged her inside the house and into the coal room. I locked the door and tried to think of what to do.

Before long, I could hear movement inside the room and figured she was awake. I went inside and she attacked me, clawing at my face, hitting me, kicking me. I pushed her and she fell. I ran to her side, took her hand, tried to help her but she started screaming. I covered her mouth with my hand to stifle her screams, but she kept struggling and trying to pull away. Before I knew it, my hands were around her neck…and then…she went still. I panicked. I didn't know what to do. I needed time to think and figure out what to do."

Ellen couldn't believe how anyone could be so callous about another life. "So, you're Stephen Mitchem?"

He didn't answer right away. She could hear him pacing. "How did you find out my name? Did you talk to my uncle? He said he would never tell anyone."

Ellen thought about what he was saying. His uncle knew he killed Jenny? "Your uncle helped you." Ellen said, hoping it would provoke him into telling her what happened.

"I didn't know who else to call. I explained it was an accident and that I didn't mean to kill her. He showed up and saw an old comforter in the basement, so we wrapped her body in that and drug it to the lake. We used a couple of big rocks to weigh the body down and then rolled her body into the darkness…" Stephen's voice trailed off.

"And Emily?" Ellen asked. Her right hand was almost free now. She just needed a little more time.

"I didn't mean to kill Jenny, but I couldn't change it. I Just wanted to get on with my life and forget the whole thing. After a few months had passed, it seemed like everyone was forgetting about Jenny. My uncle helped to cover it up and made it seem like her disappearance was a random thing."

This caused Ellen to stop struggling against the ropes for a moment as what he said sank in. His uncle had helped cover up Jenny's death and steered the investigation into her disappearance away from his nephew. The only way that was possible is if Stephen's uncle was part of the investigation. Like a cop. "Wasn't your uncle worried about his job?" Ellen asked, resuming her attempts to free herself.

"Of course he was. He took every chance he got to remind me of everything he had risked for me. But as I said, it seemed as if we had gotten away with it. Then Emily found the Goddamned locket. It must have fallen off in the basement during the struggle and somehow Emily stumbled upon it. She started looking into Jenny's disappearance. I had to stop her from ruining my life."

This guy was a complete narcissist. What about Jenny's life? Or Emily's? Ellen wondered if he ever thought about that or was he too focused on himself to consider the impact his actions had on Jenny and Emily or their families. "Did your uncle help you kill Emily?" Ellen asked.

"No. But after it happened, I called him. I threatened to reveal his part in covering up Jenny's death if he didn't help me cover up Emily's death too. He had no choice, so he drove her out and dumped her body on the side of the road and then planted evidence at that rapist's house. When Morton Stanley killed himself, it all but convinced everyone of his guilt. I got away with it and it would have stayed that way if you hadn't come along." He concluded, his voice taking on a menacing tone.

Ellen's mind scrambled for something to say to buy herself some more time. "What about your uncle? If you kill me, do you honestly think he will help you cover up my death as well?"

Stephen said, "Of course he will. He doesn't have a choice. He's the one that told me you were looking into Jenny and Emily's deaths. He even told me about the ghost you supposedly saw. Why would he tell me all that if he didn't expect me to act on it?"

The only person Ellen had shared her ghostly encounters with was Detective Crawley. Was it possible he was Stephen's uncle and had known this whole time what happened to Emily and Jenny? Ellen didn't want to believe it, but it made sense. He had been dead set against her asking questions and had done everything in his power to thwart her efforts to find the truth.

Ellen was trying to figure out a way to confirm her suspicions that Detective Crawley was Stephen's uncle when she heard the creak of a basement stair. Was someone coming? Had Stephen heard it too? Ellen couldn't be sure who it could be. She prayed it wasn't Natalie. She needed to distract Stephen. She began crying loudly and begging for her life. "Please don't hurt me. I won't say anything, I swear! I'm begging you to let me go."

Just then Ellen finally managed to slip her hands free of the ropes. At the same time, she heard a loud crash and a momentary struggle and then it sounded like Stephen cried out. What was happening?

Suddenly Ellen felt someone beside her pulling off the blindfold. It took Ellen's eyes a moment to adjust to the sudden light but as her vision cleared, she saw a very concerned Marcy standing in front of her.

"Ellen are you okay? We need to get out of here!" Marcie was saying as she helped to pull Ellen to her feet.

As Ellen got to her feet and allowed Marcie to lead her towards the door, she noticed Stephen crumpled on the ground, clutching his side and moaning. She could see blood pooling out from beneath him. "What happened?" She asked Marcie as they raced upstairs and towards freedom.

"He had a knife and when I burst through the door, he tripped and fell on the knife." Marcie explained, breathless as she threw open the back door and pulled Ellen behind her.

As the door was closing behind her, Ellen turned to look and saw Stephen coming up the basement stairs. "He's coming Marcie. Run!"

The two women ran towards the lake, hoping to get to the other side and put the lake between them and Stephen. If they could manage to do that, maybe they stood a chance.

They had just reached the opposite side of the lake when Marcie cried out, "Ellen look out!"

Before Ellen knew what was happening, Marcie pushed Ellen out of the way and Ellen lost her balance and fell backwards into the lake. Before the water pulled her under, she saw Stephen plunge the knife into Marcie's back. Ellen immediately began thrashing around, trying to pull herself back to the surface.

As her head broke the water's surface, she saw Stephen diving into the water and swimming towards her. He covered the distance in seconds. Ellen tried to turn and swim away from him, but she felt a strong hand grab her from behind and push her back down under the water's surface. Her lungs burned for oxygen, and she clawed at the hands that held her under the water, trying to break free. She dug her fingernails into the skin of Stephen's hands and arms, but it did not good. He was too strong. She was going to die.

As Ellen began to come to terms with her fate, she thought of Scott and Natalie and how much she loved them. She thought of Natalie growing up without a mother, just as Ellen herself had. She thought of Marcie and wondered if her friend was still alive. Ellen's throat ached and her lungs burned. She couldn't hold on much longer...

Suddenly, the hands that firmly held Ellen just below the water, loosened their grip and then released her altogether. Ellen clawed her way to the surface and kicked out and away from Stephen. As her head broke the surface, she saw Stephen being pulled under water, a ghostly hand wrapped around his neck. Just before they sank below the water's surface, Ellen's eyes met Jenny's. The young girl nodded once before disappearing under the water, pulling Stephen down towards his watery grave.

Epilogue

"Hey there sleepyhead. Time to rise and shine. I brought your favorite; Glazed Donuts with extra glaze." Ellen said as she entered Marcie's hospital room.

Groggy, Marcie yawned and stretched and then winced from the stiches in her shoulder from the knife wound. "Thank God Ellen! They're trying to starve me in here I tell you. You wouldn't believe what they're trying to pass off as food at this place."

Chuckling, Ellen handed Marcie the bag and said, "Can I get you anything else?"

Marcie plunged her hand into the bag and extracted a gooey donut, dripping with glaze. Taking a huge bite, she closed her eyes and said, "This is absolute heaven".

It had been two days since the events at Ellen's house unfolded and left one man dead and Marcie injured. When Ellen had finally pulled herself out of the lake and made her way to Marcie's motionless form on the bank of the lake, she had thought for certain her friend was dead. When she pressed her fingers to Marcie's neck, she was beyond relieved to feel a faint but distinct pulse. She felt Marcie's pockets, found her cell phone and called the paramedics.

In the ensuing days, Ellen revealed what she had learned about Jenny and Emily's deaths and Detective Crawley's involvement. He was arrested and charged and, pending an investigation, would likely face jail time for his part in the cover-up of the two girls' deaths. He maintained he helped Stephen to spare his sister from having to learn the truth about her son.

The lake at Ellen's house was searched and Stephen's body was exhumed. It still didn't seem real, and Ellen was looking forward to getting back to some semblance of normal.

"Have the doctors said when you can go home?" Ellen asked, taking a seat in a chair next to Marcie's bed.

"They said maybe later today or tomorrow. They want to make sure there's not any residual damage from the knife wound and run a few more tests but it sounds like I was lucky. The knife didn't hit anything vital." Marcie said polishing off the first donut and moving in on her second.

Reaching over and taking one of Marcie's donut smeared hands, Ellen said, "Oh my God Marcie, you have no idea how worried I have been. I just don't think I could take it if something happened to you."

"Hey, none of this was your fault, Ell. I want you to know that I don't blame you for anything that happened. Let's just put this all behind us and move forward. And besides," she added with a sly smile, "this scar is going to gain me some major sympathy points with Nick."

Laughing, Ellen said, "I'm looking forward to putting all this behind us too. No more killers or ghosts or unsolved mysteries for me."

And she meant it...at the moment.

Made in the USA
Las Vegas, NV
22 January 2022